"What about Victoria?"

The suspicion in Thane's eyes was obvious. "You've come to take my daughter away, haven't you, Sapphira?" he continued. "To deprive me of her."

"Why?" Sapphira blazed back at Thane, suddenly alive with a heady courage. "Would you give me your son?"

"No!" Thane's breathing was heavy, his fingers biting into the thin flesh of her arms. "No," he repeated softly. "If that's what you were hoping, forget it. Stephanos is mine by law—and he remains mine!"

"Take your hands off me!" Sapphira was shocked at her own courage and amazed when he obeyed.

"As a matter of fact, you're quite wrong," she told him with a calmness she didn't feel. "I haven't come to ask for custody of our son—I'm prepared to give up my right to custody of our daughter."

Angela Wells left the bustling world of media marketing and advertising to marry and start a family in a suburb of London. Writing started out as a hobby, and she uses backgrounds she knows well from her many travels for her books. Her ambitions, she says, in addition to writing many more romances, are to visit Australia, pilot a light aircraft and own a word-processing machine.

Books by Angela Wells

HARLEQUIN PRESENTS
1164—LOVE'S WRONGS
1181—ERRANT DAUGHTER

HARLEQUIN ROMANCE
2844—MOROCCAN MADNESS
2903—DESPERATE REMEDY
2921—FORTUNE'S FOOL
3006—STILL TEMPTATION
3054—RASH CONTRACT
3143—SUMMER'S PRIDE
3167—ENDLESS SUMMER

Don't miss any of our special offers. Write to us at the following address for information on our newest releases.

Harlequin Reader Service
P.O. Box 1397, Buffalo, NY 14240
Canadian address: P.O. Box 603,
Fort Erie, Ont. L2A 5X3

ANGELA WELLS

tattered loving

Harlequin Books

TORONTO • NEW YORK • LONDON
AMSTERDAM • PARIS • SYDNEY • HAMBURG
STOCKHOLM • ATHENS • TOKYO • MILAN
MADRID • WARSAW • BUDAPEST • AUCKLAND

Till whatsoever star that guides by moving,
Points on me graciously with fair aspect,
And puts apparel on my tatter'd loving,
To show me worthy of thy sweet respect:
Then may I dare to boast how I may love thee...

–William Shakespeare
The Sonnets

Harlequin Presents first edition May 1992
ISBN 0-373-11462-1

Original hardcover edition published in 1991
by Mills & Boon Limited

TATTERED LOVING

CHAPTER ONE

SAPPHIRA wore white: a simple dress with rounded neckline, capped sleeves that masked the angular joints at the tops of her arms and a slightly gathered skirt that softened the too slender outline of her hips. Despite the shimmering heat of the early afternoon the colour of the material had proved most efficient in deflecting the needle-sharp rays of Greek sunlight as she'd walked like an automaton through the deserted streets.

In fact, she was aware of goose-pimples on the pale exposed flesh of her arms and of a persistent shiver that chilled her spine.

She wore white—but it should have been black, she thought with the strange detachment which seemed to have taken over her being since the Deed of Settlement had been decided. Black, the colour of mourning: for hadn't she already lost nearly everything in the world that she'd once lived for? And wasn't she now on her way to give up the last remaining bond left to her?

The walk would stabilise her, give her time to rehearse what she was going to say to Thane. There would be no tears or accusations, she'd determined grimly. She'd lost so much, but at least she'd regained some of her shattered pride. It had taken her a trio of sleepless nights to realise and accept the truth, to absorb the pain and make her agonising decision.

Turning away from the road, she made her way down a dusty path fringed with long grasses and wild flowers not yet dried to straw by the unremitting power of the early season sun. Reaching the villa, her feet took her unerringly through the beautiful casual garden with its flagged courtyards on different levels, its riot of hollyhocks, dahlias, roses and gladioli, beneath stone columns entwined with ultramarine convolvulus, magenta bougainvillaea and orange trumpet vine, leading her under an archway festooned with vines to the large double olive wood front door.

She paused, blonde head dipped, its plait of silver fair hair fastened severely in a coronet on her crown, exposing her fragile neck, as she took off the large sunglasses that had masked her face to search the contents of the small bag she carried over one shoulder.

Her jaw clenched in sudden exasperation as her fingers stabbed convulsively at the bag's soft leather. Once more she'd been trapped by the force of habit! Fool that she was, in that instant she'd forgotten that she could no longer come and go as she pleased through the Villa Andromeda. Once she'd been its mistress. Now she was only a visitor.

Taking a deep breath, she abandoned her futile search for the key she no longer possessed, snapping the bag shut and pressing the doorbell with a confidence she was far from feeling.

'Kyria Stavrolakes...' The greeting from the middle-aged woman who opened the door was a quaint mixture of pleasure, sadness and embarrassment as Sapphira acknowledged her presence with a slight dip of her fair head as if it was the most normal thing in the world to await an invitation into one's own house by one's own servant. Except, of course, she was no longer welcome in the house...and Ephimi's allegiance was pledged solely to Thane.

'I believe the *kyrios* is expecting me, Ephimi?' Her voice was well modulated, light and pleasant as she stepped into the cool hall, the maid closing the door behind her.

She could have said 'my husband' or even 'Kyrios Thane'. Instead she'd chosen the most formal mode of address open to her. Formality and politeness were the order of the day, overt emotion and hysteria—the outward show of passion—things of the past. To know passion one had to be alive, and since the court's decision she had thought of herself as dead in every sense of the word except the biological, her blood turned to metaphorical ice by a ruling which, to her Anglo-Saxon sense of justice, had been as bizarre as it had been uncontestable.

'If the *kyria* would like to wait...' Ephimi was clearly ill at ease, seeing the incongruity of asking Sapphira to wait in what had been her own sitting-room. Biting her lip in distress, she hurried on, her pleasant face agitated. 'I don't think the *kyrios* expected you quite so early. He's only recently finished lunch and I believe he's taking a shower.'

'There's no hurry.' Sapphira walked stiff-backed, with the elegance of a princess, towards the sitting-room. 'Perhaps you'll let him know I'm here when he's finished.' To her distress her mind involuntarily conjured up an image of Thane, naked and vulnerable beneath a cascade of water. No, not vulnerable. That suggested weakness and there was nothing weak about the man she'd married. It had been his strength, his single-mindedness of purpose which had drawn her to him that evening five and a half years ago.

She'd been seventeen and it had been Christmas Eve.

Seating herself on the edge of one of the long, sumptuously upholstered pinewood settles in the quiet room, her mind drifted backwards to that meeting in England's pretty West Country. She'd been out with the usual crowd from the local art college where she had been studying textile design. They'd hired a minibus to bring them home from the end-of-term Christmas party and she'd been flushed with champagne, riding on a high of goodwill to all men, when she'd burst into the darkened lounge of her home expecting to find it deserted, only to be greeted by her brother.

'David, darling! I thought you were spending Christmas with Marcia!' Her surprise at seeing him had made her oblivious to the other figure which had risen to its feet at her bold entrance. She'd gazed up into her sibling's face, her brow wrinkled with concern lest his presence meant some personal disaster.

'So did I,' he'd agreed ruefully. 'But it seems she can't get any time off until Boxing Day, so I thought I'd spend a couple of nights with the family, and, what's more to the point, I've brought a friend to share the celebrations with us.'

'Lovely!' She'd dimpled up at him, full of laughter and the spicy, racy excitement of being young and healthy and full of life, with the expectation of a fun-filled holiday ahead of her. 'My very first Christmas present this year!' Aware now of the other presence in the room, she'd turned to greet the visitor.

Her first mistake had been to assume that the new-comer would be David's age. He wasn't. David had been twenty. The stranger had been nearer thirty, she'd assessed as he had moved forward and she had been able to see his face more clearly. Certainly he was no boy. Perhaps he'd never been one, if being boyish meant being pubescent and gauche and spotty, she'd thought inconsequentially, wishing she'd been less flip with her greeting as sombre eyes took their toll of her. There had been nothing disrespectful in the surveillance she had received so why had she begun to regret her choice of costume for the party?

Ondine, spirit of the lake, she'd decided, congratulating herself on thinking of something which was both easy to make, imaginative in concept and attractive to wear. Over a flesh-coloured body-stocking she'd arranged flowing strips of chiffon silk in pale greens and blues. Interspersed amid the floating effervescent drift of colour were strips of silver lamé, glistening and twisting in the light, and through her waist-length, ash-blonde hair she'd woven thin cords of silver thread.

At the party her outfit had met with universal acclaim. Now, in the presence of this looming sage-eyed god whose steady gaze threatened to destroy her poise, she suddenly felt infantile and unsophisticated. It was his eyes that were her undoing: the irises the soft yellow-green of a tropic river teeming with life yet placid in the midday sun, the white clear against the tanned skin, the whole extravagantly lashed and set in deep sockets.

'Sapphira,' David was saying, oblivious to the trauma she was undergoing. 'This is Athanasios Stavrolakes. He's been observing and participating in some of our engineering computer sciences research at New College. As he's going to be in England over the holiday I thought he'd like to see how we celebrate.'

'In Greece our major festival is Easter.' His voice was low and deep with only a trace of accent to betray his eastern Mediterranean origin, and those incredibly compelling eyes had smiled at her.

'Yes,' she said, dredging up some long-stored memory in an effort to impress this imposing stranger. 'Yes, I know.'

She felt faint as he moved closer to her, taking her hand in a clasp of friendship.

'Sapphira,' he said gently, turning her name into a forbidden caress so that she trembled at his daring, her heart beating with a painful urgency as his eyes had spoken a message she didn't dare to translate, travelling with considered judgement over the length of her body from crown to silver-painted toe, returning to gaze directly into her light blue eyes now apprehensively wide beneath the sweep of darkened lashes. 'Not one of the more usual English names, surely? Or am I more ignorant than I supposed?'

Ignorance was the last state she would ever accord to this man, she'd thought wildly. If intelligence and its application marked a man, then Athanasios Stavrolakes was indelibly branded!

'It's Biblical in origin,' she returned primly. 'My father tends to shun the innovative. Sapphira was the wife of Ananias.'

'Ah, yes.' He confirmed her first impression by inclining his dark head knowledgeably. 'The man who lied and paid the price of his deception with his life. If I remember correctly, his wife shared his fate.'

'A harsh judgement for loyalty, I've always thought!' She faced him defiantly, intent on defending the woman whose name she bore. 'If I loved a man I, too, would back him even to the grave!'

How empty and cruel that claim seemed now—but then she had meant every word of it. Untouched and untried by love's sword, she had been an innocent fool!

'Lucky man.' His riposte had been swift, his beautifully curved mouth lifting into a smile as his eyes dwelt on the challenge mirrored on her face. 'But today you aren't portraying your unfortunate namesake, I see. You are, perhaps, a water-lily?'

'No!' She laughed, glad of the opportunity to release some of the tension building inside her. 'I'm a nymph—a water sprite.'

Their eyes met and held as Sapphira felt herself drawn into a magnetic field where fantasy was stronger than reality.

'And perhaps *you* are *my* Christmas present, *ne*?' he asked, his expression quizzical.

Oh, good heavens, she'd thought, stricken, suddenly remembering her brother's presence, whatever would David think of this flirtatious interchange between strangers? But he'd turned away and was pouring himself a drink, muttering something about the trials and tribulations of having a girlfriend who was a staff-nurse in a hospital.

She smiled politely, ignoring the question, aware that her brother's acquaintance was the most beautiful man she'd ever seen. Not male-modellish beautiful—something too cruel about that glorious mouth, or was it the downward lines that grooved his cheeks that hinted at devilry rather than sainthood? As for his eyes—a girl could drown in those dark fringed pools and wake up stranded on a far beach without visible means of support!

Scarcely knowing what she was doing, Sapphira drifted her gaze in a clean sweep downwards, embracing good shoulders encased in a formal white shirt, a firmly muscled chest, a trim waist and legs which possessed a length of thigh she'd ignorantly supposed inapplicable to the Grecian race!

'One can perhaps change a Christmas gift if it doesn't come up to standard?' His voice was deceptively soft as his eyes glittered like diamonds, hard, brilliant and obsessive.

'Some people would,' she agreed lightly, wishing her heart would cease its abnormally fast rhythm and allow the tremor which had seized her hands to subside. 'But we have a saying here that it's the thought that counts.'

Slim and elegant as a ballerina, she stretched, deliberately encouraging her muscles to relax. There was nothing unusual in her parents' agreeing to house an unexpected guest. After all, their four-bedroomed house could easily be adapted to accommodate one more by the simple means of Sapphira giving up her usual bedroom and moving in with her elder sister, Abby. 'I expect David has already told you which room you'll be having Mr Stavrolakes...?'

His dark head, the thick hair springing strongly to set off the broad forehead, dipped briefly in acknowledgment. 'I shall be sleeping in your bed, Sapphira—if you have no objection?'

'Take it—it is yours!' Some far memory of Greek hospitality prompted her airy response, but she hadn't been able to suppress the tiny shiver of anticipation which had curled down her spine. It had been almost as if she'd said *take me, I am yours!*. 'May you enjoy sweet dreams, Mr Stavrolakes.'

'Thank you.' But he didn't smile and she was left with the impression that he knew the passage of her thoughts and wasn't surprised. 'Since I am to share your festival with you, perhaps I can persuade you to call me Thanos?'

'Thanos...' She repeated the name, her head a little to one side. 'Rather unusual and *very* attractive...'

Some deep instinct had warned her then that she was playing a dangerous game by this overt teasing of a man whose maturity and experience was so far advanced of her own, but at seventeen she'd been too young and protected to realise exactly how stimulating her posturing and posing were to the attractive Greek, whose steady contemplation encouraged her to self-indulgence.

She'd been sounding out her newly discovered sexuality against a seasoned and mature master and she'd been green, oh, so green, as she'd laughed into his still face, her eyes dancing with amusement. 'But I think *I'd* like to call you something a little different, something special just between you and me ...'

No reply. Just a leisurely lift of one eyebrow and that continuing evaluating look which had brought an unexpected tension into the pleasant room. Taking his silence as agreement to her suggestion, Sapphira had announced her decision. 'Thane, then. I shall call you Thane!'

At the time she'd had no idea why the name should have sprung so readily to her mind. Later, intrigued by the power of her own subconscious, she had looked it up in a dictionary. "One who is the owner of land given for bravery and personal service to the King," she had read. "A man who ranks between ordinary freeman and hereditary peers." Thane. Lord ... liege ... master.

With a conscious effort she dragged her thoughts away from the past. The Villa Andromeda had been built into the side of a hill on the outskirts of Kethina, a small town not far from Athens, so that, gazing through the opened glass doors, she could look down over the tumble of terraced gardens to the neighbouring smallholdings. How still and quiet everything was, as if life had been held in temporary suspension, so that her present suffering was in a vacuum. Restlessly, she let her eyes wander around the pleasant room in which she sat.

Nothing had changed since her decision of nine months ago to move out of the villa and make Lorna's flat her residence. The cool mosaic floor was spotless, the pinewood furniture with its tasteful upholstery could have been positioned for a *Homes and Gardens* supplement, the walls with their arches and alcoves were as pleasing to the eye as they'd ever been. Why *should* there have been changes? she asked herself, facing reality with a stab of pain. It wasn't as if she'd ever contributed anything more than a few superficial touches to the smooth running of Thane's household. He employed the efficient and hard-working Ephimi to minister to that element of his creature comforts.

Her own contribution to Thane's life had been specialised and unique... or so she had once thought. A feeling of desolation passed through her as she tightened her fingers round her bag as if seeking comfort from its presence on her lap. She'd always loved this gracious room. She would miss relaxing in its welcoming ambience.

A movement of the latch on the door forewarned her of Thane's arrival. As her body slewed round to face the opening, her bag slipped from her nervous clasp to spin across the sparkling mosaic beyond her reach. Her jaw tensed in anger at her own clumsiness. One momentary lapse of concentration and her carefully assumed dignity was shaking like Knossos before the destruction of the Minoan society!

Straight-backed, she dropped carefully to one knee to retrieve the recalcitrant white leather, counting up to three slowly, taking the added time to gather her senses, before rising gracefully to her full height to stare into the hostile face of the man who stood watching her with the brooding look of a male Nemesis about to pronounce judgement.

He looked the way Lucifer must have done after that final shattering interview with God, she thought, allowing herself the luxury of meeting his appraisal with the unfaltering attention of her cyan eyes, bemused that he alone of everything had changed when she'd imagined him the most adamantine force in the house! Now there was an added darkness beneath his eyes, a hint of pallor beneath the tanned skin, tiny lines of strain that marked the corners of his generous, passionate mouth.

Yet some things remained the same: the pride and antagonism in the bearing of his formidable body, the thrust of his jaw and the continuing lack of pity which left his features without tenderness or understanding. Indomitable, she thought with a little shiver impossible to hide; yes, that was the word. How poetically apt that she'd unwittingly knelt at his feet a few seconds ago. A Freudian slip of action, if there ever was one! Thane. Lord...liege...master.

Unexpectedly, she swayed, the room turning into a tunnel of rushing darkness which replaced Thane's implacable face as a soft moan escaped her lips. She sensed rather than saw him close the distance between them, knew, from the warmth and tangy scent of freshly showered male that enveloped her at the instant her legs could no longer support her, that she'd been swept up into his arms and spared the discomfort of toppling to the hard floor.

She never lost total consciousness. Even before she'd been lifted with effortless efficiency on to the settle, the oxygen had begun to recirculate in her brain. To think she'd imagined herself prepared for the impact of meeting Thane in these conditions. Clearly, she'd underestimated the power of his presence, or perhaps the extent of her own frailty!

'Here. This may make you feel a little stronger.' He held a crystal balloon of brandy within easy reach of her fingers.

'Metaxa? For me?' Her spirit resurging, her eyes sparkled a challenge at his saturnine countenance. 'But surely, St Domenica's Day is in January, not June?'

With a sick excitement she saw his knuckles whiten as his fist tightened round the reflective surface of the glass. Good, her barb had reached him! It seemed he hadn't forgotten the last time he'd seen her with a drink in her hand, when he'd baited her with a biting sarcasm that she appeared to treat every day as St Domenica's feast! The reference had eluded her and he'd had to explain with a cold superiority that he was alluding to the occasion when Greek women celebrated Midwife's Day.

'It has the dubious reputation of being the only day of the year when our women may drink a little more than is good for them, and not be criticised for their excess,' he had told her pointedly. It had been an unmerited jibe, and had hurt her deeply. True, she admitted, it was at a time when she'd taken to having a small glass of brandy each night before going to bed to help her sleep, but she hadn't expected to be branded an inebriate, and the implied insult still rankled.

'So you remember that?' He looked musingly at her defiant face as his initial tenseness relaxed. 'You surprise me, Sapphira. I thought you found the customs and culture of my country too boring for your attention.'

'I think one always remembers an injustice,' she responded tautly. 'I've never been bored by Greece.'

'Just by the Greeks then—or, should I say, by one Greek in particular?' His expression taunted her, inciting her to an angry response.

Aware of the danger, she drew in a deep breath, deliberately controlling her emotions, proud of the drawling composure of her voice when it emerged from between her dry lips. 'If that's what you choose to believe.' Her shoulders hunched dismissively. 'I've no wish to argue with you.'

'A definite improvement in outlook!' Blandly, he proffered the glass to her once more. 'In that case, take your medicine—and smile!'

'No—no, I can't.' Hastily she held up a palm in refusal. 'It wouldn't be wise to drink on an empty stomach, especially in this heat.'

'You've had no lunch?' Irritation drew lines of annoyance across Thane's broad forehead, every inch of his arrogant body demanding that she answer him.

No lunch, no breakfast, no dinner the previous evening. The list was a long one if she cared to detail it, which she didn't. Food had become of minor importance to her during the last three days. The less she ate, the less her body required. She shrugged careless shoulders, achingly aware that Thane was regarding her with critical attention, his angry eyes travelling with an unflattering thoroughness over her too-slender frame.

'I didn't feel like eating,' she offered indifferently, hoping he'd let the subject drop. 'Sometimes the heat affects me like that.'

'Hmph!' With a grunt of impatience, he set the glass of brandy down on the table at her side, before striding to the door to summon Ephimi, his voice carrying imperiously down the silent hallway. 'Some delicacies for my wife to eat, immediately, please. Something to tempt a flagging appetite...'

Powering back into the room he stood before her. Six feet three inches of dominant manhood that she'd once found the most tempting entity her narrow world had ever produced! Now, looking at him gave her no pleasure. All that was left of what she'd once fondly believed was love was a dull ache, which had become an integral part of her existence over the past few months.

'Ephimi will bring you a snack,' he told her curtly, sage eyes glittering, daring her to defy him. 'You'll pay me the courtesy of eating it, please, Sapphira, since to defy me out of principle would be irresponsible in the circumstances. If you have no fears on your own behalf from passing out at the wheel of a car, at least consider that you will have my daughter with you!'

He was tense and unhappy, too disturbed to settle down, prowling like a caged animal, hands thrust into the pockets of his pale slacks, tightening the fit across his lean buttocks. His strongly muscled shoulders hunched forward as he stalked with a feral grace before her, his thickly matted black hair clinging to his well-shaped skull in springy waves that defied the severity of the styling he'd tried to force upon them.

'I didn't drive here. I walked.' She made the announcement calmly, feeling a stab of triumph when her casual confession pulled him up short in his paces.

'Walked!' he hurled back at her. 'For the love of God, *yineka*! All the way from the town? In this heat? No wonder you look half dead!'

'Thank you, Thane.' She offered him a little twisted smile, not hurt by his uncomplimentary comment, since it was the simple truth. Every morning, the mirror in Lorna's spare bedroom confirmed her complete lack of attractiveness: the gaunt face, the hollows above her breastbone, the scrawny, pale arms that had once been the graceful, curving limbs of a water sprite...

'So what are your plans?' Thane demanded harshly. 'Is the ubiquituous Michael playing chauffeur—or do you intend to get a taxi?' Then, as she didn't make a direct answer, his brow darkened. 'You don't expect me to drive you, do you?'

Instinctively Sapphira cowered from his controlled fury, shrinking back into the comfort of the thick cushions behind her. As if she would demean herself by asking a favour from him! Even seeing him alone like this was an ordeal she was facing only because her own sense of personal honour demanded she must.

'I don't expect anything from you,' she told him with an icy dignity, 'I intend to return in the same way I came.'

'On foot!' he exploded, his dark voice curdled with anger. 'With a three-year-old child?' Before she'd realised his intention, Thane was approaching her with swift strides, lifting her to her feet and supporting her by grasping her upper arms as he stared down into her ashen face. 'You do mean to take Victoria with you, don't you, Sapphira? You *have* come to deprive me of my daughter, have you not?'

'Why?' she blazed back at Thane, suddenly alive with a heady courage. 'Would you give me your son?' Head flung back, she faced him with blatant bravery, her beautiful light blue eyes sparkling a dangerous challenge directly into his level stare.

'No.' Thane's breathing was heavy and controlled, his fingers biting into the thin layer of flesh on her gawky arms. 'No,' he repeated softly. 'If that was what you were hoping for, forget it. I would never, ever give you my son. Stephanos is mine by law—and he remains mine!' There was a terrible agonised beauty in the dark face that dared her to lie to him. 'Is that why you came here? To plead with me about Stephanos?'

'Take your hands off me!' Sapphira was shocked at her own courage, and amazed when her harshly voiced instruction was obeyed. Automatically she raised her hands to touch the tender skin that had suffered his attack, observing how his eyes clouded over as he perceived her action: with remorse? Or irritation perhaps? It was hard to tell.

'As a matter of fact, you're quite wrong,' she told him with a calmness she didn't feel. 'I haven't come to ask you for *our* son. On the contrary, I've come to tell you I'm prepared to give up my right to custody of *our* daughter.'

She paused, not for dramatic effect, but because she found the words so difficult to say. 'You can have both children.'

CHAPTER TWO

SHE had practised her speech all morning, so there was no reason why she should start to cry. Heaven knew she was unattractive enough without pink eyes and a red nose. Besides, Ephimi had appeared at the door with a tray bearing plates of assorted fruit, eggs and cheese, slices of freshly baked bread and fingers of cake, and was looking at her with dismay etched all over her pleasant face.

Dabbing hastily at her eyes with a quickly found tissue, Sapphira saw Thane relieve Ephimi of her burden with a word of thanks.

'Eat, Sapphira.' Crisply, he commanded her obedience in a tone that pre-empted argument.

Silently she lifted one of the plates, inviting him to take first choice.

'Thank you.' He acknowledged her gesture formally but without genuine gratitude. 'But I have no hunger.'

His rejection came as no surprise. It had been a long time since they'd eaten a meal together, and even longer since they'd completed one without rancour and bitterness adding their unwanted flavour to the repast. Reluctantly she helped herself to a finger of cake. It was still warm from the oven, dissolving in her mouth without effort.

'So.' It was Thane who broke the silence between them, his hostility apparent, not only in the coldness of his voice, but in every line of his body. 'You have decided to abandon both your children. Strange; the only thing I never doubted about you was your love for Victoria

23

and Stephanos. Who talked you into that idea? Your liberated friend or her conniving brother?' Bitterness lent a thread of anger to the deep timbre of his voice.

'It was my decision.' She wouldn't let him see how painfully his scorn seared her sensibilities, or how the derogation of her friends offended her. 'And they're *our* children, Thane, not just *mine*!' she corrected him with quiet dignity.

'Ah, yes.' Thane's glittering gaze pierced her own as if trying to bore into her mind. '*Our* children. One for me and one for you by kind permission of the law. The Judgement of Solomon, Sapphira—and you're turning your back on it. Why? Because you've decided to live in sin with your boyfriend? You intend to abandon them both, to seek your own satisfaction at their expense, is that it?'

'For pity's sake, Thane!' Anger rose to suppress her misery. She'd thought he would have been so delighted to have custody of both the children that he wouldn't have stooped to insulting her. She should have known better. 'You really don't understand, do you?' She allowed her eyes to dwell on his proud face, rigid with accusation, seeking any glimpse of comprehension and finding none. 'This has nothing at all to do with Lorna or Michael. Lorna only wants my happiness, and Michael has never been anything more than a friend who just happens to be a man!'

Nothing in his expression changed, and she knew her protestation had fallen on ears which elected to be deaf. In the face of such intractability she sighed. 'It's not that I don't want Victoria...' Her voice broke momentarily to be brought under immediate control. 'Of course I want her—I want them both! But they're twins...twins! Can't you see what that means? If you'd ever watched them together—really watched them—you'd know that

their need for each other is far greater than their need
for me! Judgement of Solomon!' Her bitter laugh rang
round the room. 'In England, I would have been given
custody of both of them. What kind of arbiter would
dream of separating twins—dividing them between their
parents? It's the devil's work, and I can't allow it to
happen!'

'In Greece, one doesn't take a son away from his
father!' There was no apology on Thane's stern face, as
the lines round his mouth deepened with stress. If eyes
were truly the mirror of the soul, then Sapphira was
looking into a secret place which held its own core of
agony, and for a moment she felt a deep wash of pity
invade her. Only in her darkest moments had she ever
doubted Thane's devotion to their children.

'You believed all the time that you'd be awarded
custody of *both* of them,' she said dully, facing the
knowledge fully for the first time.

'Yes.' He admitted it tautly. 'Yes, I did. Here, at least,
a man is always head of his own household, responsible
for his own flesh and blood.'

'Well, now you've got your wish.' Unable to sit still
any longer, Sapphira rose to her feet, smoothing the
creases from her dress with slender, agitated fingers.
What a short-sighted fool she'd been not to realise how
differently the law might operate in the eastern
Mediterranean. She'd actually believed she'd won a
victory when Thane, after months of adamantly refusing to consider the divorce she'd demanded, had suggested a legal separation.

If she hadn't been so distressed at the time, she might
have realised that he was expecting custody of the
children—just as she had been. Instead there'd been this
crazy, obscene ruling for the separation of the twins,
who, although fraternal as opposed to identical, had been

companions since birth, sharing a bond so close, so special that no one could observe them together and not be aware of it . . .

'Have I?' Thane pulled himself to his feet and followed her to where she stood gazing from the window. 'Why do you suppose I refused you the divorce you kept pleading for? Certainly not so you could relinquish all your responsibilities! The fact is you're their mother, Sapphira. Nothing can ever change that—regardless of how we now feel about each other. And you're wrong to say they don't need you. If you really believe that then you've let your infatuation for Michael West blind you to reality!'

'I'm not infatuated with——'

She had been about to say 'with anyone', but her protest was cut short by Thane's guttural sound of disgust.

'Spare me a description of your emotions. I'm not in the mood to tolerate it. Just because it's impossible for us to live together as man and wife there's no reason why our children should be deprived of your company, or not know and accept you as their mother. So if you have other ideas you'd do well to forget them—unless you also want to forget the generous settlement our lawyers worked out on your behalf!' His voice deepened with disgust. 'Somehow I don't see you happy employed as a kitchen hand in order to make ends meet!'

There was no reason why fear should tighten her muscles into a nervous spasm, unless it was the awareness that Thane was a formidable antagonist, possessed of an uncanny power and determination to get his own way against all the odds.

'Well?' he prompted irritably, watching her thoughts leave their mark on her face. 'I want the truth, Sapphira.

Do you intend to desert our children? Is that what's behind your visit here today?'

She lifted her blonde head proudly, scathing him with the coolness of her beautiful eyes. 'No, I have no plans to move out of their life. I still want to exercise my rights to see them as often as possible.'

'Ah.' It was a sound of triumph rather than relief, as if she had succumbed to his threats of impoverishing her. Well, she could put him right about that!

'As far as the settlement is concerned,' she battled on doggedly, 'I shall support myself by whatever means possible as soon as I'm able to find employment.'

'That won't be necessary!' He glowered at her. 'My offer to the court was made without duress. As far as I'm concerned you are still nominally my wife and as such I shall support you—while you continue to cherish our children.'

Sapphira made a small gesture of despair with both hands. 'I appreciate your generosity, but I'm not a gold-digger, Thane. It seems unfair that you should continue to provide for me when——'

'When I no longer have the right to enjoy your body?' he cut in sharply.

'Yes . . . no . . .' Confused, she made herself meet the magnetic force of his eyes, seeing too the harsh twist of his lips which should have been humorous—but wasn't. It had been many months since he had enjoyed her body, a chasm of dull grey days when she'd felt no joyous upsurge of flesh or spirit at his presence. Yet once, not so long ago, he'd been both her adoring slave and munificent master.

'Oh, this is an impossible situation!' she cried out in sudden anguish. 'A divorce would have been a much cleaner solution for both of us!'

'Not by my standards.' Curtly he contradicted her. 'I'm a man of my word and I promised to take you for better or worse until death, did I not?'

'Things change...' She looked away, unable to bear the pain of his unjustifiable censure. Thane had also promised to love and cherish her and that didn't include making love to her sister or taking Angelia Andronicos as his mistress!

'But not everything.' He regarded her steadily. 'So you still intend to live close by when I can find you a suitable property, and see the twins regularly?' As she nodded, he persevered. 'You have no intention of returning to England, and forsaking your visiting rights altogether?'

'No...' She pictured the animated faces of the children, their soft arms and eager voices, their undemanding love and choked on the lump forming in her throat. 'There's nothing for me in England now.' Not since you drove a knife of hatred between my only sister and me, she could have added, but didn't.

'You can have unlimited access,' Thane assured her roughly. 'It was never my intention to prevent you from seeing them—although I would have fought with everything I had to prevent your taking them away from me!'

'Strange, isn't it?' Sapphira's sweet pale mouth curved into a slight smile. 'We were both so sure of our unassailable rights, and in the event the officials made fools of both of us.'

'*Paliatsos*, huh!' Thane used the Greek work for clowns. 'It's not a role I'm used to playing.' There was a flash of anger in his low voice that boded ill for the authorities who had sought to deprive him of custody of his daughter. If he'd been an Olympian deity he would no doubt have directed a thunderbolt on those worthies as a warning to amend their judgement, such was his bearing in that instant of outrage.

'Well, you can shed the ginger wig and red nose now, can't you?' Sapphira offered with painful humour. 'You've got everything you wanted after all.'

'Not everything—but enough for the moment,' he snapped, his brow furrowing. 'I suppose you're waiting for me to thank you?'

'What for?' Wearily Sapphira turned away from the window. 'My decision to forgo my rights has nothing to do with you, only with the children's welfare.'

'In that case you'd better go and tell them.' He gestured upwards. 'They're in the nursery. I tried to explain to them that when you came this afternoon you'd be taking Victoria back to Kethina with you, but I have to admit I didn't get very far.' Self-mocking amusement softened the startling clarity of his light eyes. 'They have an amazing way of ganging up and refusing to accept what they don't want to happen—our precocious *didimee*.'

Recognising the Greek word for twins, Sapphira smiled involuntarily, glad that Thane, too, was aware of the strong psychological link between their offspring and didn't put down her observations to an over-strong imagination!

'I'll go and confirm their expectations, then,' she said lightly, suppressing a tiny pang of hurt that her daughter had had no wish to go with her. If she'd had any doubt about the rightness of her sacrifice this was the confirmation she needed.

'Disappoint them, you mean.' Thane moved in front of her, courteously opening the door for her to exit. 'The last I heard they were both making plans to go with you.' His face was bland as she turned astonished eyes to his countenance, wondering if he were joking at her expense; but no. There was nothing on those classically hewn features to suggest any such thing. But then, in victory, Thane had always been generous.

Hesitating outside the nursery door, Sapphira heard the childish laughter and the lower, more guttural sound of Spiridoula's Greek. Perhaps, she thought wearily, if her own Greek had been better when Thane had first introduced the young village girl into the nursery, or if Spiridoula had had the faintest knowledge of English, then there might have been more of a rapport between them. As it was she'd read Spiridoula's taciturnity as hostility, and her silences as dumb insolence. Only Thane's insistence that she was competent and devoted to her charges, despite her youth, had guaranteed her continued employment. Now, over three years later, Sapphira was prepared to admit that time had proved him right. Certainly Sapphira herself would never have moved out of the family house nine months ago to lodge with Lorna unless she'd been satisfied that the children would be well looked after in her nightly absences should the need arise. Not that she had let a day go by without visiting them—except, of course, when she'd known Thane would be there...

'Kyria Stavrolakes...' Spiridoula acknowledged her entry into the room with a sharp nod of her raven head.

'*Herete,* Spiridoula.' Sapphira smiled pleasantly, glad that her perseverance with the Greek tongue over the past months was beginning to pay dividends.

'Stephanos is coming with us too, Mummy!' Victoria, ever the more boisterous and talkative of the twins, flung herself at Sapphira, expressing herself in a mixture of English and Greek which, despite his wife's defection, Thane had obviously continued to encourage.

'Can we bring some of our toys? Daddy says I must take all my clothes—can Stephanos bring all his too? Daddy bought me a new dress specially to wear today, but I chose it. It's white, see!' She pulled enthusiastically at the pretty cotton broderie anglaise, 'Like a wedding dress. I'm going to marry Kostas but Daddy says I shall have to learn how to cook moussaka first because it's a woman's duty to feed her husband.'

'Trust Daddy to get his priorities right,' Sapphira murmured, not in the least surprised by this evidence of her estranged husband's chauvinism, hugging her small daughter before turning to hold out her arms to her son.

Quieter and less effusive than his sister, Stephanos more closely resembled his father in looks. Born by Caesarian section, he had been the first recorded birth. Not for the first time did Sapphira wonder whether it had been a conscious decision by the medical team to deliver the male first. Despite becoming a full member of the European Community the historical background of the Greek patriarchal society was still very much in evidence—as she had just learned to her grief...

'Daddy said he'd be lonely here without me.' Solemn eyes stared into her face. 'He said that we can't always do what we want to...and he'd take me to the seaside instead, but I want to come with you and Vicki...can't you make him say "yes"?'

'It wasn't really Daddy's decision, sweetheart.' She gave the lithe body a quick cuddle as Victoria wriggled away from her. 'In any case,' she added brightly, seeing puzzlement cloud the little boy's face, 'there's been a change of plan. Both of you are staying here with Daddy and Spiridoula, and I'll come and see you as often as I can. We'll be able to go out just like we do now and have a lovely time together—you'll see.'

'You never come and tuck us in any more and last night Vicki was sick and cried for you!' Stephanos accused sulkily.

Oh, dear God! Sapphira felt her heart plummet. Clearly the child was all right now, but what of the future? Suppose she was really ill, sick with one of the childhood infections? How could she bear to be parted from her... from either of them? Even knowing Thane and Spiridoula would do their utmost wouldn't be enough to give her ease of spirit...

She fought down the wave of nausea that threatened to choke her as Victoria intervened chattily, 'Doula says I had too much fizzy lemonade to drink. Do you have to go away every night? Daddy doesn't. But he did last night. He didn't want to because I was sick and Angelia came and looked at me and said she'd stay with me so's Daddy could go because it was 'portant, but Doula said I'd be all right!'

'Kostas's mummy goes out every night,' Stephanos volunteered. 'She works in a taverna and earns lots of money because Kostas's daddy can't buy them everything they want. Is that what you do?'

What to tell them? Despite their apparent precociousness, it was difficult to judge just how much they understood. Besides, what had Thane already said to them, if anything? Your mother and I can't live together any more. We don't love each other. We don't want to share a house or a bed. We don't want to be seen together, that's why I take Angelia Andronicos out. Angelia is experienced, you see, a widow who understands that a man has needs...

Abruptly she stopped fantasising. Whatever the truth of the matter, Thane was hardly likely to communicate it to his children in such uncompromising terms!

'No, I don't have to go out to work,' she told her son. 'But I've got a very good friend called Lorna who's invited me to stay with her for a while.'

'But you are coming back to us soon, Mummy?'

It was Victoria who asked the question she'd been dreading. All these months and they'd seemed to accept her coming and going at intervals. In her heart of hearts she'd known it was only a matter of time.

'Oh, I shan't be far away,' she prevaricated quickly. 'In fact, we've got lots of plans to make. It could be quite exciting for all of us!' She tried to infuse a note of optimism into her opinion which she was far from feeling.

'Are you still cross with Daddy?' Stephanos challenged her unexpectedly.

'No, of course not, I...' Confused, she could only think that it would be wrong to agree to any state of affairs which might worry them.

'You used to shout at him!' Again, the accusation from the small stubborn face of her son.

'He used to shout at Mummy!' Victoria interposed, seemingly unconcerned. 'Doula used to put the music on ever so loud but you could still hear him!'

Her quick wits came to Sapphira's aid, as, forcing herself to laugh, she moved towards the door. 'People's voices always get louder when they're excited or happy, don't you know? It doesn't mean anything. My heavens! You ought to hear the both of you at times. I wonder poor Spiridoula hasn't gone deaf!'

'Deaf, deaf, deaf!' chanted Victoria, clearly delighted with the explanation, and raising her own voice several decibels.

'Hush!' Sapphira reprimanded sternly, but was unable to keep the small smile of relief from her mouth. 'Why don't we all go downstairs to the garden?'

'Are you going to stay with us now, Mummy?' Stephanos touched her hand as he asked the question.

'Oh, my darling, I don't think I can...' Distress was mirrored in her face as she opened the nursery door. 'Daddy wasn't expecting me to stay and Lorna...'

'Lorna can always be phoned.' Thane loomed into view taking her by surprise. 'I wondered what you were all talking about up here?'

He made it a question as if he suspected her of undermining his authority, of lying about him, of trying to put him in a bad light in front of his children. How could he be expected to know she would never sink to such depths? Whatever Thane had done or not done it was between the two of them as husband and wife.

'As a matter of fact, there are several things we need to discuss,' he added curtly.

'Surely they can wait?' Tiredness was creeping up on Sapphira, exacerbated by the nervous strain she was under.

'No, I'm afraid not. You see, much as I appreciate your gesture, I wasn't expecting it and it raises some problems.' He ushered the children downstairs, standing back to allow Spiridoula to precede him, before taking Sapphira gently by the arm.

'Come back into the sitting-room. You can watch the children playing outside in the garden and we can talk.' He looked at her, his eyes narrowed calculatingly. 'Come, Sapphira, you're no longer afraid to be alone with me, are you?'

Silently she shook her head. In this man's presence she had suffered every emotion known to womankind. Now there was none left. She allowed him to lead her where he would.

'Do you remember Konstantinos?'

The curt question took her by surprise. 'The island in the Cyclades? Yes of course. We went there the first summer after we were married.' She smiled unrestrainedly as memories of the three weeks spent there flooded back. 'We stayed in that old farmhouse you told me you bought when you started to become successful and needed a place to escape to when the pressures of work became too much for you.' She paused, the smile still playing round her lips. 'You said I was the first woman you'd ever taken there...'

'The only woman,' he amended softly, as she seated herself half-turned from him so she could watch the activity in the garden. 'I'd decided to take Stephanos there for a few days while I work on compiling a particularly complex program which is giving us all a bit of a headache at the moment.'

'So?' She didn't want to remember the halcyon summer days they'd shared on that tiny speck of heaven, *sans* airstrip, *sans* made-up roads, that only the most discriminating tourists had discovered. The memory of those glorious hours only served to make her present plight the more agonising, and she failed to see what concern it was of hers where Thane intended to go, anyway.

'So...I can manage one child, but not the two of them when I'm working.'

'Ephimi——' she began.

'Has already arranged with me to spend some time in Neapolis with her brother who has recently arrived on a short visit from the States.'

'Well, Spiridoula...'

'Has been forbidden by her fiancé to share a house on a lonely island with a man who has recently separated from his wife without a chaperon being present.'

'Oh.' That chauvinistic decision would obviously become law to the young Greek girl and wasn't worth debating. Thane had a point, Sapphira admitted—not that she doubted his capabilities of organising the twins into the Spartan discipline he would need to enable him to concentrate on the complicated flow charts which formed an integral part of his work, but it would take time and energy he wouldn't be prepared to expend.

Stephanos, the quieter and more intense child, separated from his sister would have been amenable—but Victoria...Sapphira smiled ruefully, trying to imagine Thane attempting to curb his daughter's youthful exuberance without female aid.

'So you want me to keep Victoria for a few more days?'

'On the contrary.' He hesitated just long enough to give added emphasis to his next words. 'I want you to come with us.'

'That's ridiculous!' She stared at him aghast. 'How can I possibly go anywhere with you? I'm your ex-wife!'

'Estranged wife,' Thane corrected her coolly. 'That doesn't mean we can't co-operate if it suits both our purposes, does it? The court has set us boundaries, true, because we asked it to do so, but if we decide by mutual agreement to cross them we shall not be penalised, *ne*?' He raised a dark eyebrow, inviting her comment, continuing unperturbed when none was forthcoming. 'Presumably you've just told the children they're staying together. Since Stephanos knows I intended to take him to Konstantinos, Victoria will have assumed that she, too, will be enjoying a stay at the seaside. The solution is therefore simple.

'Since you will be with me, Spiridoula's boyfriend can hardly object to her accompanying us. She can take major responsibility for the children and you and I can go our own ways. Besides——' he passed a totally encompassing stare over her, from her startled eyes past her shock-parted lips, to the nervous crossing and uncrossing of her slim ankles, '—you look as if you need a holiday.'

'But we can't share a house again!' Desperation sharpened her voice.

'Why not?' The stubborn set of his jaw challenged her. 'If you recall, the place is large enough to accommodate all of us with room to spare. There's no need for us even to speak to each other if that's how you prefer it. Just think of the advantages—Spiridoula's boyfriend will not be jealous, I shall have the peace and quiet I require for my project and you,' he paused slightly before continuing, 'you, Sapphira *mou*, will have a few precious days and nights with both your children before you relinquish them forever to my care.'

'Thane!' His name on her lips was half protest, half prayer. How could he be so cruel as to taunt her with her loss? And yet others might argue he was being generous in allowing her a last period of self-indulgent motherhood. He had even addressed her in Greek as 'my Sapphira' as he had done in the joyous days of their short courtship. Dared she allow herself to be seduced once more by his silver tongue?

Yet the benefits to herself were obvious—the time with the children, an opportunity to try to get them to accept that by moving out she wasn't abandoning them, that she had wanted them as much as their father had but had been crushed by the power of the courts and had acted only in their long-term interests...

'Why do you hesitate?' he encouraged her softly. 'Are you afraid of me? Do you not trust me to honour the terms of our separation?'

Sapphira's eyes flared wide open in distress. How could she answer such a question? She knew her estranged husband as a proud and passionate man, adamantly opposed to her wish to break every legal tie between them, not because he loved her but because having once possessed her his pride demanded he keep dominion over

her, even if it meant sharing his name, his property and
his income with a woman he no longer loved.

'So that's it.' Whatever Thane had read on her face
appeared to supply the answer he'd demanded. She
watched, speechless, as he ran his tongue slowly across
his upper lip before speaking again. 'Have you still not
realised that you have managed to do what no other
woman has ever attempted, *agape mou*?' he asked her
gently, his eyes gleaming with ill-disguised hostility. 'You
have robbed me of my manhood. I am less now than
the predatory beach boy or amorous waiter who may
throw a hopeful arm round your shoulders.

'I have been forbidden by law to lay a finger on you
whether it be in anger or in passion. I, who have held
you in my arms and carried you to my bed, imprinted
you with my body and impregnated you with my seed;
I, the man whom you promised to love, honour and obey
for eternity, am threatened with imprisonment if I so
much as lay a finger on your delicate skin. Do you imagine the lure of your flesh is so great that I would voluntarily languish in a prison cell for the joy of touching
it? Do you, Sapphy *mou*?'

'No...' Sapphira's eyes closed self-protectively to cut
out the vision of his bitter face and the glimpse she had
caught of herself in the long wide mirror which gave
space and depth to the pleasant room. She could feel
that same flesh to which he'd so cruelly referred cringing
beneath his scorn. If she'd ever been vain, that sin had
been eradicated once and forever since the twins' birth.

Even her own eyes shrank from the vision of her over-
thin body and bony limbs. She had no pretensions about
her own attractiveness, particularly not to a man like
Thane whose classic masculine beauty was linked to a
sharp intelligence and a simmering sensuality which made

him outstanding among his peers, and hadn't she the evidence of her own experience to confirm his distaste?

She felt her cheeks colour with embarrassment. 'No,' she whispered. 'I don't think that.'

'Then it's the opinion of your anaemic compatriot which bothers you, and that of the *maliosa*—his sister!'

'Lorna is no witch—she's the truest friend I've ever had!' Indignation spotted her pale cheeks with scarlet. 'Insulting her does you no credit. She offered me sanctuary when to stay near you was impossible!' She drew in a deep breath, aware of the hard core of temper which had tightened Thane's jaw to steel, but still determined to make her point although reason told her she was beating her head against a brick wall to expect his understanding. 'And as for her brother—well, Michael may not possess the obvious charisma of a Stavrolakes male, but he's kind and considerate and loyal, and has no influence over my decisions. Despite what it pleases you to believe, he isn't, never has been and is never likely to be my lover!'

'Is that so?' He regarded her flushed face thoughtfully. 'I do hope so, Sapphy, because you'll never bear his legitimate children while I have the power to prevent it!'

'The only children I shall ever want are the ones I already have.' Wearily she rose to her feet. 'Or perhaps I should say—the ones I once had...'

'Then prove it, Sapphy! Show me their welfare means more to you than the opinion of the *maliosa* or the man you've just disclaimed as your lover.' With two quick steps he blocked her exit from the room. 'If you're as devoted to Stephanos and Victoria as you assert, surely you can be unselfish enough to let them enjoy one last family holiday?'

CHAPTER THREE

'YOU'RE mad, quite mad!' Lorna West declared succinctly, standing with hands on slim hips, regarding Sapphira as she packed a small suitcase with smooth efficiency. 'You've gone through all this pain, all this trauma so that you never have to set eyes on the man again and now you propose going on holiday with him?' Her voice rose in querulous amazement. 'Honestly, Sapphy, you need your head examined.'

'Well, it wouldn't be for the first time, would it?' Sapphira asked, a faint smile lifting the contours of her shapely mouth.

'And it's no good trying to make me feel guilty,' Lorna shot back sternly, 'by referring to the sessions you had with a psychiatrist while you were in the clinic, because it won't work. We both know that your illness after the twins were born was physical, caused by an imbalance of hormones, as all the medical evidence went to show. This time it's different. This time your judgement appears oddly warped!' Her tone softened. 'I truly do have your best interest at heart, you know.'

'Of course I know.' This time Sapphira's smile was full and genuine.

Meeting Lorna when she had had been a turning point in her recovery, Sapphira was sure of it. Lonely and unhappy, in a deep state of depression, her mind filled with thoughts of her failed marriage and her own sister's treachery, Sapphira had found that Lorna's appearance in her life had given her the stimulus she'd needed to recapture her interest in the future.

Of course the treatment she'd received during her three-month stay in the clinic had aided her physical recovery, but it had been Lorna's cheerful companionship which had boosted her psychological outlook. Thane had arranged for all her meals to be sent in to her from a high-class restaurant in the vicinity. Beautifully cooked and served and of infinite variety though they were, Sapphira had had little appetite for them until the day that Lorna herself appeared with her dinner.

It had probably been because she was English that Lorna had managed to break through the reserved air Sapphira assumed. The joy Sapphira felt at being able to talk in her own language and at length to a woman who was both vibrant and amusing, who listened as well as talked, who was both warm yet sensible, had been the spiritual tonic she'd so much needed.

Lorna's appearance as a waitress had been a one-off event in a staffing emergency, but to Sapphira's delight she had returned time and time again as a visitor until a strong friendship had been forged between them. By the time she was discharged from the clinic Sapphira had learned all about Lorna's life, and how, leaving her job in a London advertising agency in order to escape from a love affair which was going nowhere, she'd made a temporary home in Greece, using her abilities to promote the restaurant in Kethina which was owned jointly by her younger brother Michael and a local Greek businessman.

In her mid-thirties, Lorna was a striking woman, positive and sure of herself and her own capabilities, and as physically removed as possible from the cruel description of 'witch' bestowed on her by a man who, mistakenly, saw her as a rival for his wife's loyalty.

Who else would have given her sanctuary for the past nine months while she and Thane were waiting for their separation to be made a fact of law? If only for that, Sapphira knew Lorna deserved as full an explanation as she could give her.

'It's entirely different now, Lorna,' she said patiently. 'Thane fully accepts that he has no jurisdiction over me. As he pointed out himself, if he lays a finger on me I can have him sent to gaol. At the worst we're strangers— at the best, friends.'

'Friends!' Lorna made no attempt to hide her scorn. 'Good grief, my dear, if you really believe that passion can become friendship because a court of law has decreed it, then you're in a worse state than I supposed. And as for gaol...' She paused dramatically. 'You and I both know that you lack the determination to see Thanos Stavrolakes behind bars—and if we both know it, do you think he doesn't?'

'You may be right,' Sapphira admitted grudgingly. Only a sadist would cage a king of the beasts and she'd always abhorred cruelty in any shape or form. 'But Thane has his own code of honour——'

'Seducing your sister and flaunting a mistress before your eyes?' Lorna's raised eyebrows mocked her.

'I could never prove either of those things!' Sapphira defended herself quickly. 'If I'd been able to I could have got a divorce and I wouldn't be in the mess I'm in now. But in any case they have no bearing on the present. I trust him not to break his word not to molest me.'

'You may be right.' Lorna's grudging agreement took Sapphira by surprise. 'If he overstepped the mark you'd probably be able to wrest custody of Stephanos from him. He won't have overlooked that!'

Neither did he desire her any more, Sapphira shuddered. He'd made that abundantly clear the last time she'd shared his bed.

'Well, there you are, then.'

'And how about you, Sapphy?' Lorna asked kindly. 'Are these idyllic days with the twins going to make it easier for you when you finally have to say goodbye?'

Defiantly Sapphira faced her friend. 'Isn't there a saying—why worry about tomorrow, it may never come?'

'Oh, my dear——' Lorna shook her head sadly. 'In my experience it always does.'

'Then I'll face up to it when it arrives,' Sapphira declared stoutly, refusing to admit the element of truth in Lorna's remark. She'd been unwilling at the start but now she realised that the companionship of her children for a few days of uncomplicated pleasure was a bonus she couldn't turn her back on.

'So be it.' Lorna gave in gracefully. 'You'd better take lots of sun cream with you. The mixture of sun and wind in the Cyclades can turn a peach into a prune.' She cast a knowledgeable eye over Sapphira's hair. 'And treat yourself to a good coconut oil shampoo while you're at it or you'll end up looking more like Worzel Gummidge than the Sleeping Beauty!'

'It's a bit late for that, I think!' Ruefully Sapphira ran her fingers through her hair, hating its dry brittleness.

'Rubbish, it's never too late to make improvements, and at your age the results of some self-indulgence will work miracles in a very short time.' Lorna cast critical eyes over the other girl's figure. 'There's not much wrong with you that a little pampering won't put right. Leave it to me—I'll pack you a beauty kit that will metamorphose you. In return, all I ask is that you feed yourself properly, if not lavishly, when you get there! OK?'

'All right.' Sapphira gave in gracefully. She owed too much to Lorna to take a stand against her instructions. They were well-intentioned and would do no harm even if they did little good.

Packing her suitcase, she allowed her mind to dwell on the events of the afternoon. Following her agreement to Thane's plans, she'd stayed longer with the children than she'd originally intended, sharing an early supper with them, enjoying their chatter about the coming holiday. Thane had soon disappeared to the room he used as a study, appearing again only when she'd announced to Ephimi her intention of leaving. Despite his earlier avowal of not being prepared to drive her back to town he'd been waiting outside the front gate in his dark blue Mercedes, pushing the passenger door open as she moved towards him.

She wanted no favours from him. Instinctively she had opened her lips to tell him she preferred to walk. If he'd suggested driving her back, she would certainly have refused the offer. Instead he had taken that option away from her. Now her insistence on walking would have made her appear churlish, put her in the wrong. Besides, if she were honest with herself, the long walk through the dusty streets held little attraction for her. If Thane could change his mind, then she could change hers, she supposed. So she'd taken her place beside him with a murmur of thanks and been gratified to see his eyebrows rise with unspoken surprise at her silent compliance. There was a great deal of satisfaction in realising that he'd been prepared for a verbal fight and that she'd robbed him of the pleasure of crossing swords with her.

She smiled to herself at the memory as she closed her suitcase. Perhaps if she'd been less keen to oppose him on other small issues over the five years of their marriage life would have been a lot easier for both of them. Strange how being given a longer leash of freedom by the courts had dulled her need to take advantage of it!

By the time she'd had a leisurely bath and washed her hair Lorna reappeared laden down with jars and bottles.

'Moisturiser, night cream, eye-gel, hand cream, high-protection sun anti-wrinkle cream, hair conditioner...' she intoned, arranging the relative containers on the dressing-table.

'Good heavens!' Laughter bubbled up inside Sapphira. 'I must be in a worse state than even I thought! Do all those things really work?'

'Most of them to some degree, I'm sure,' Lorna gave her qualified approval. 'Of course what we really need is someone to invent an anti-gravity cream. Until that happens I'm afraid the spectre of the wrinkle will continue to haunt us—that doesn't mean its arrival can't be delayed. And don't forget nature didn't intend your English rose skin to be exposed to this climate. Take them, Sapphy, with my love, and enjoy using them. After all, time's going to hang heavy on your hands. I doubt that Konstantinos is a hive of activity after dark so you can amuse yourself applying your own beauty treatments in the long warm evenings!'

After her friend had left her alone Sapphira opened the jar of moisturiser, and applied some of it to her face. Lorna meant well and she owed it to her friend to accept and use her gifts, despite her own inclination to let nature take its inexorable course.

Later, trying to relax beneath the cool cotton sheet on her bed, she found sleep impossible to capture. Following the process she'd been taught in the clinic, she made a deliberate effort to untense her muscles starting from her toes and working up to her neck and head. Inevitably her mind began to wander as her conscious control slipped, fleeting incidents from the past skimming before her until, inevitably, she was drawn back to that time five and a half years ago when it had all begun.

It had been an hour before midnight on Christmas Day, and at her instigation, that she and Thane had first kissed.

'There's something I have to show you,' she'd told him pertly, leading him away as they all vacated the table after the celebration evening meal to make their way to the sitting-room, where, despite the comparative mildness of the weather, a traditional fire blazed in the open hearth.

Earlier that morning she'd broken off a large sprig from the thick bundle of mistletoe gracing the pendant light in the hallway, pinning it strategically over the doorway leading to the spare room downstairs which doubled as a study and games-room.

'There's an old Druid custom,' she told him serenely, pointing to the cluster of green leaves and translucent berries, aware that every nerve in her body was tingling and her heart was tripping a light fast rhythm as she took his hand and felt his fingers curl possessively around her own. 'As long as there are berries on the stems a man can stand beneath it and steal a kiss from a woman, but every time he does so he has to pluck one of the berries. When they've all gone, so has his right to—to touch her!'

'And she has no right to refuse him?' His expression was just the right balance of scholarly interest and masculine calculation to raise her blood pressure by at least one point.

'Well, not if she happens to be standing right beneath it,' she teased him, eyes widening in tremulous expectation. Surely he wouldn't be so churlish as to refuse to honour the traditions of his host country?

He wasn't. His soft green eyes alive with amusement, he accepted the offer of her tender lips as she parted them instantly beneath the warmth of his caress, inviting him to invade her, reaching for the thickness of his hair with her pink-tipped fingers, pressing her body intimately against him, filling her senses with the electrifying quality of his masculinity.

'Sapphy—oh, Sapphy...' His mouth was hot velvet on her cheeks, on her nose, devouring her soft lips with a heated passion, seeking out the sweetness of her mouth, possessing it with the thrust of his tongue. Glowing all over, exulting in the subtle change she could detect in her own body, she had responded to his caresses with unrestrained enthusiasm, rising on tiptoe and moving against him, enjoying the effect her closeness was having on his male hormones.

When his hands moved down her body, tracing her shape with fingers which trembled, she sighed her pleasure, feeling sensations that she had never known before. He was everything she had dreamed of—handsome, gentle yet dominant, taking charge of the situation she had engineered, turning a harmless pagan custom into something much more dangerous as the full awareness of her own desire burst upon her.

'Sapphy...' He held her tightly, his breathing heavy, his voice husky as he released her mouth. 'Dear God—Sapphy!'

'What is it? What's wrong?' Anxious to prolong the pleasant feelings which had made her whole body tingle with a heady expectation, she searched his face, afraid in her immaturity that she had done something wrong.

There was no amusement on his face now as he stared down into her open gaze with eyes that smouldered with an inward heat.

'Nothing,' he assured her thickly, staring down into her upraised face. 'I had no idea that the Druids had such...interesting customs.'

'Sapphy—where are you?' It was Abby's voice, breaking the trance which had held her captive in his arms. Instantly she detached herself, still tremulous from the fervour Thane's embrace had conjured up, too unsure of what had happened between them to advertise it to a third person, however dear.

'David wants to play charades. Are you coming to join us?' As Abby's voice reached its highest volume she arrived in their presence, a faint flush of embarrassment colouring her cheeks as she observed her sister and brother's friend beneath the mistletoe. 'Oh, I'm sorry,' she stumbled unhappily, 'I thought...'

'Your sister was explaining to me the charming custom of the mistletoe,' Thane interposed easily. 'You permit, yes?'

Moving away from Sapphira, he had taken Abby's hand, guiding her beneath the doorframe. She'd watched her sister's pretty face grow even pinker as the tall Greek had lightly touched each soft cheek with his lips before solemnly detaching two further berries from the plant above his head.

For the first time in her life she'd experienced a surge of jealousy against the older girl. Despite the five-year age-gap between them they'd always been the closest of friends and confidantes. Abby with her light brown curly hair and hazel eyes had never been short of boyfriends, although there'd been no one serious in her life to date, and Sapphira had never envied her her easy familiarity with members of the opposite sex. In fact she'd been proud of her sister's popularity.

Thane's salutation had been cursory and inoffensive, taking the tension away from the situation she had contrived, but, oh, how she had hated Abby at that moment for coming in and spoiling everything! Had it been then, at that instant, that Thane had first been attracted to her sister? At twenty-two Abby had been much nearer his own age, plus the fact that she had the sophistication and self-assurance that earning one's own living bestows on an adult!

Rather sulkily, Sapphira had joined the other members of the family and their guests to spend a couple of hours playing the traditional charades before announcing her intention of going to bed, where sleep had eluded her aroused yet unsatisfied body.

The following days had been a heady mixture of intense pleasure and abject frustration for her as she had shared Thane's company with Abby and David. He desired her—she knew he did! Yet he was subtle, never embarrassing either her or her siblings by obvious flirting, but she sensed it in the seemingly accidental brushes of their bodies, in his slow sweet smile reserved specifically for her, the language of his eyes when they met her own, and the snatched intimacies of conversation they enjoyed.

'When am I going to see you alone again, Sapphy?' He had followed her into the dining-room, where she was laying the table for lunch on New Year's Eve, closing the door behind him and leaning on it, defending it from unwelcome intruders.

One part of her knew her mother and sister were in the kitchen preparing to dish up the meal while her father and brother were idly watching television in the large sitting-room, but the other knew that there were only two people in the world at that moment—Thane and herself.

'Do you want to?' She was young enough to be coy, glancing at him from behind lowered lashes while her blood thundered in her veins and her body flushed with internal warmth. 'I thought you were enjoying the company of David and Abby?'

'When, Sapphy?' He refused to respond to her teasing, his burning regard consuming her from head to toe as if he already owned her. A trickle of trepidation shivered down her spine. This was no uncertain youth she could manipulate. This was a man who could devour her, consume her and leave only ashes as evidence of his power. Now was the time to refuse him if that was what she wanted . . .

Artlessly she licked her lips because the skin felt painfully dry and saw his pupils darken as his eyes followed the movement. In a few moments they would be surrounded by her family, laughing, joking, warmly affectionate, the strong, loving bastion which had supported and protected her all her life. She must make her decision now—or lose him for ever because he had already announced his imminent plans to return to Greece and the thriving business he was building up from scratch.

'Tonight,' she said, her voice scarcely more than a whisper. 'Mum and Dad are going to a New Year's party at his office, Abby's been invited out to dinner, and we could make some excuse not to join David and his girlfriend Marcia at the hospital "do".' She smiled. 'I'm sure they won't miss us.'

Over five years later she could look back at her youthful self and cringe at her own naïveté. But then she had had no doubts. Over the preceding days she'd come to know a lot more about Thane and his background. He was the youngest child and only son in a family of four children, and all his sisters were married and had families of their own.

His father had died seven years previously and his mother five years later, by which time he'd graduated from university where he'd studied computer sciences and joined a company specialising in providing custom-made programs for engineering. From there it had been an obvious but major step to set up his own business in partnership with an equally ambitious fellow countryman.

But the most important thing as far as she'd been concerned was that he had been unmarried, nor would he lay claim to a girlfriend, fending off her curiosity by explaining that, with a working day sometimes twenty hours long, he'd had no time for relationships which demanded commitment.

Dear Lord, how she had wanted him to be her first lover! Full of romantic notions, she had wanted to surrender her virginity to a man who would temper power with tenderness; a man who would initiate her into the ultimate of the erotic arts with power and persuasion, who would make this milestone in her life a memorable one on which she could look back with pride and pleasure...

Thane had pleaded the need to revise his course notes before returning to his homeland; she had declared the start of a migraine. It had been as easy as that.

Alone in the house, they had made love on the carpet in front of the fire. She had ached for that mythical creature, the perfect lover—and Thane had not disappointed her.

Wordlessly he had unclothed her, his mouth following the passage of his hands as sensation followed sensation, bringing gasps of gratification to her lips. Selflessly he had pleasured her, introducing her to the delights latent in her own body, worshipping her with his hands and mouth, making her his creature, so that there was nothing she wouldn't have done for him.

Reaching to embrace his body with tentative hands, she had been overwhelmed by the intensity of his response, filled with a sense of wonderment at her own power over his quickening flesh. Exploring his nakedness with an awesome joy, her breasts achingly heavy from his caresses, she had begged for his possession, sobbing out his name.

The memory of her shamelessness returned to haunt her, but stalwartly she refused to flinch from it. In the beginning she had been the architect of her own misfortune. For what happened that night she had already absolved Thane from all blame.

He had taken what she had offered so willingly, with a power and a passion which made her teenage dreams pale by comparison, as she matched his fierceness, shocked yet delighted by his total abandonment. As an initiation into the art of love it had to have been supreme. With no experience with which to compare it, Sapphira had only known that the act of love in which she had shared had been both more violent and more totally fulfilling than anything she had ever imagined.

At that moment of intense satisfaction she had believed that she was totally and irrevocably in love with the glorious Greek who had changed her from a child into a woman.

Afterwards Thane had been silent, holding her quiescent in his arms for several minutes before rising to his feet and re-dressing himself with a quick efficiency.

Full of a delicious languour, she had remained in front of the fire, pulling herself upright into a sitting position, letting the warmth from the flickering flames caress her bare back, experiencing an intimate delight in watching his positive yet graceful movements as he covered his nudity.

She was still sitting there, unselfconsciously naked, her long hair trailing over her shoulders, her shapely legs curled beneath her, when without any warning the sitting-room door was thrust open.

'What's this? Hide and seek?' It was her brother's voice; then light flooded the room and David's mouth gaped in astonishment as he stood on the threshold absorbing the scene before him.

He'd been more surprised than shocked, Sapphira was to realise later, and her own embarrassment and annoyance had been more due to the sudden breaking of the fairy-tale spell than the fact she was disrobed.

Of the three of them, it had been Thane whose reactions had been most quickly triggered. With a quick movement he had come to stand in front of her, masking her from David's curious gaze.

'Look, I'm sorry, but I didn't expect, I mean...' Apology and indignation mingled in the younger man's tone. 'There was an accident on the motorway and Marcia had to go on duty...'

'No, it's I who should apologise,' Thane had interrupted firmly. 'It would appear that I have abused your hospitality but I beg you will understand and forgive me when I tell you that Sapphira and I are going to be married.'

She'd been overjoyed, convinced he loved her as much as she loved him. It was only later, after the twins were born, that she realised she'd been living in a world of illusion. Thane had married her out of a misplaced sense of honour and responsibility. Rather than offend the laws of hospitality, the adherence to which had been ingrained in his character since birth, he'd tied himself to a woman whom not only did he not love, but whom over the months of their union—and despite its fruitfulness—he had grown to despise.

CHAPTER FOUR

'WE'LL get a taxi to the house,' Thane announced, shading his eyes and looking down the unmade road which led from the tiny harbour, while Stephanos and Victoria peered excitedly into the clear sea lapping round the small jetty. 'The island's still only got one, but he still comes to meet the afternoon ferry. Are you feeling all right, Sapphira?' His curt enquiry was accompanied by a quick speculative look, as she pushed a wayward strand of fair hair off her damp forehead.

'Yes, I'm fine.' A little tired perhaps but that was only because of the tension of sharing his company when she'd conditioned herself to banish him totally from her life. Of course she would have exercised her prerogative to visit the twins, but her visits would have been arranged to avoid coming face to face with their father... So much for the best-laid plans of mice and men, she thought with a wry acknowledgement to the poet. How could she have foreseen a situation like this a couple of days ago?

'The rest will do you good,' Thane spoke abruptly.

'We'll probably both benefit from a little peace and quiet,' she agreed politely, surprised and gratified that they could speak to each other at a civilised level like normal human beings. If he kept his distance as promised, the coming days might be more beneficial to her than she could have dared hope when he'd first astounded her with his suggestion.

'It's the taxi, Daddy!' Stephanos jumped up and down in excitement as the ramshackle vehicle loomed in on them out of a rising cloud of dust.

'So it is, *hios mou.*' A careless hand ruffled the boy's thick dark hair. 'Not long now.'

Ten minutes later Sapphira was absorbing the view of the old farmhouse with hungry, reminiscent eyes, and a deep ache wrenching at her heart because the past could never be recaptured, and in these particular circumstances her memories were agonisingly poignant.

Nothing had changed. The stone walls were picturesquely covered with whitewash flaking artistically beneath the shimmering salute of the sun: green shutters protected open windows, tamarisks and jacarandas lent their welcome whispering shade to the flagged terrace which surrounded the building, and from where she stood she could see past the side of the house to the rough ground beyond it: the simple shower standing like the focal point of an oasis surrounded by tubs of shoulder-high flame coloured cannas; and, only a few yards beyond, the small sandy bay and the shining sea.

Taking a suitcase in each hand, Thane led the way to the front door indicating with a nod of his dark head that the two women and the children follow him.

'I want to go in the sea! Mummy, can I go in the sea?' Victoria tugged at her mother's hand as Sapphira lifted the remaining case.

'When we've unpacked and found your swimsuit, darling.' She smiled down at her happy daughter.

'That shouldn't take long.' Abandoning his burden at the foot of the stairs, Thane lifted the little girl into his arms, extending a hand to his son. 'We'll go up and find which room has been prepared for you, shall we? And then we'll see where Mummy and Spiridoula will be sleeping.'

'You seem to be very well organised,' Sapphira commented, following in their wake as they mounted the wide wooden steps.

'Of course.' Thane's tone was smug. 'I don't like leaving things to chance. Although I haven't been back here since our honeymoon I pay an agent to keep an eye on the place. When he knew my plans he arranged with a local girl to make it fit for habitation, stock up the cupboards, prepare the rooms and all that kind of thing.'

'It wasn't our honeymoon.' As soon as the words were out of her mouth Sapphira cursed her stupidity. What on earth had made her pick up such a minor point? Almost as if she'd suspected some camouflaged attack in the casual statement.

'How prosaic you are, Sapphy!' He was mildly chiding, but she detected a gleam of satisfaction behind the assumed innocence of the gaze he turned on her as they reached the top of the stairs and he pushed open the nearest door. 'It may have been four months after we were married, but it certainly felt like a honeymoon to me—and you too if I correctly recall your behaviour at the time.'

To her chagrin Sapphira blushed: a deep, emotionally painful response of shame at this reference to her youthful exuberance, her whole-hearted abandonment in the arms of the man she'd innocently assumed would be her partner for life, mortified that he would dare to goad her with memories she'd hoped she'd buried for ever in her subconscious.

Blithely unconcerned by her reaction, Thane cast an appraising eye round the room he had revealed. 'Ah, two single beds—this is your room then, *angellos mou*.' He smiled down at his 'little angels', the picture of the devoted father. 'And who will sleep next door to you, I wonder?'

'I shall—oh!' Sapphira bit back her claim as Thane pushed open the adjacent door to disclose a large, plainly furnished room, the centrepiece of which was a double bed.

'I'm flattered.' Calmly Thane took her suitcase from her unresisting hand and carried it into the room, placing it on the woven cover which adorned the bed. 'I had wondered if you would turn your back on the bedroom we once shared in the same way as you've chosen to turn your back on the outcome of our union.'

His lips twisted in the parody of a smile as he spoke in English, presumably so that Spiridoula, waiting patiently behind them and unused to the language, should not suspect anything untoward from his attitude, but his eyes were cold as malachite as she gasped her outrage at his condemnation.

'I'd forgotten about that—as I've forgotten everything else about that holiday,' she averred quickly. 'I don't mind where I sleep—provided it's not with you.'

'Have no fear. I have every intention of respecting your claim to newly embraced celibacy. Since you deny all knowledge of the layout of the place, may I remind you that there is a large room downstairs off the main living area? I've already arranged for it to be turned into a working-cum-sleeping area for myself.' He paused, fixing her with an ironical stare. 'Believe me, the tasks I have to do will be time-consuming enough to keep my libido in check. Both you and Spiridoula can sleep easy in your virginal beds content that they will remain unsullied from any approach by me.'

Turning away, he switched into rapid Greek, addressing Spiridoula with the easy charm that had once personified his actions, guiding her from the room to the one across the passageway, leaving Sapphira clenching her teeth with indignation at the way he had chosen to reassure her.

Still, there was no point in brooding about it. Far better that she let his snide remarks ride over her and hope he would soon grow tired of trying to needle her with images of his past virility when she didn't respond.

Systematically she began unpacking her case, neatly putting away the small selection of casual clothes she had brought with her. The only incongruous item was the apricot-coloured satin nightdress Lorna had thrust upon her earlier that morning.

'It's all part of the therapeutic treatment, Sapphy,' she'd insisted. 'If you love yourself and dress to please yourself, you won't be dependent on anyone else's affection to keep sane and healthy!'

It hadn't been a point worth arguing, and since she'd had no wish to hurt her friend, Sapphira had accepted the luxurious garment with genuine thanks for the other woman's thoughtfulness.

Thankful that the bedroom contained its own shower, she cooled off beneath its welcome spray before changing into a simple cotton crêpe dress, the colour of which matched her eyes. She'd spoken truly when she'd denied memory of the room, but only because she'd been so determined to stake her claim to major responsibility for her children during these few precious days that she'd scarcely paid attention to where she was.

Now she remembered only too clearly.

Walking to the window, she gazed out across the tumble of stones and rough grass which lay beyond the property's boundary and which gradually gave way to a fine silver sand beach. Spiridoula and the children were already at the water's edge engaged in a boisterous game of water splashing. They were so beautiful, her *didimee*, so strong of limb and firm of flesh, so full of vitality.

How could she ever regret the long days when, suffering from toxaemia, she had lain in darkness, half-drugged in a hospital bed to ensure their survival? They were perfect, and if necessary she would have sacrificed her life to achieve that result!

Damn it, she hadn't intended to cry! Furiously she wiped the back of her hand across her eyes. They were happy. Of course they were! They loved their father and Spiridoula and Ephimi. Who could doubt her decision? A nagging doubt forced itself to the front of her mind. Had she been selfish in accepting Thane's suggestion to come here with them? Already their routine had been disrupted by her sporadic absences. Once she'd made her decision, wouldn't a clean break have been better for them?

Too late to regret her decision now. To rescind it would cause even further upheaval. With a sigh she turned from the window. Since she'd decided on self-indulgence she would make the most of it and join the happy party on the beach.

Since she had hoped to escape from the house without encountering Thane, her heart sank as, reaching the bottom of the stairs, she saw him emerge from the door leading to the sitting-room, a tall glass containing an iced liquid in one hand.

'Perhaps you could spare me a few minutes of your time?' he enquired smoothly. 'I'm sure you're anxious to know how easy I'm going to make it for you to avoid me, and I'd like to put your mind at rest. Can I offer you a drink?'

She hesitated for only a moment, seduced by the thought of liquid refreshment, and he was right, they did need to arrange some kind of routine.

'Orange juice?' she suggested, and watched as he procured a bottle from a small refrigerated cupboard, tipping its contents into a glass and adding ice.

Broad shoulders eased beneath the navy cotton shirt that stretched across his well-developed muscles as he handed her the drink. '*Yassou,*' he murmured with ironical courtesy, lifting his own glass to salute her, watching while she took her first sip before moving away.

'I hope you're not disappointed that I haven't had the place modernised,' he said abruptly. 'But it always seemed to me that most of its charm was in its simplicity.'

'Simplicity?' she echoed, unable to curb the sudden laughter in her voice. 'Showers, fridges, interior-sprung mattresses?'

He had the grace to smile, his eyes running over her in a way that sent the warm blood pounding through her veins. 'Comparative simplicity, then,' he corrected himself. 'I admit I have made a few improvements to indulge my sybaritic nature—but very few. No television or washing machines or air-conditioning, no expensive artefacts or furnishings. The basic construction of the place hasn't been altered. It's still recognisable as the farmhouse it used to be before the young men left to seek their fortunes on the mainland and the ground reverted to nature.' He paused, then added quietly, 'I've been approached by a property dealer who wants to turn it into holiday apartments.'

'But you won't sell, surely?' Her eyes widened as her voice deepened in dismay.

'Why not?' He shrugged his shoulders. 'If the price is right I should be a fool to refuse.'

'But I thought you loved the place...' She stopped in mid-sentence, reminding herself that what he did was no longer any business of hers.

'Love...' he repeated the word thoughtfully. 'But that's just a matter of interpretation, isn't it, Sapphy?' He stood watching her, his face set in grim, almost accusing lines.

'I—you ... that is, we were going to discuss some kind of routine.' Resolutely she decided that she wouldn't rise to any of his baits. It was a long time since she'd possessed the spirit to challenge him on his own terms. Instead of the heady power she had once felt in his presence, all she felt now was weary and vulnerable.

She saw his eyes narrow in disapproval of the way she'd reverted to the original subject and felt her stomach muscles tighten in panic. He had declared himself disarmed by the decree of the court but there was no obvious sign of emasculation in the proud lift of his head or the carriage of his superb body, and the expression on his haughty face dared her to take his subjugation as a fact, even while the sweet curves of his sensuous mouth proclaimed it so.

'Ah, yes.' It was truly the smile on the face of the tiger—benign yet watchful, intrinsically threatening. 'If your forgetfulness of the bedroom we once shared hasn't extended to the kitchen where you once prepared our meals, you'll recall that facilities, although adequate, are hardly cordon bleu standard.'

'I don't recall doing much cooking,' she admitted, then regretted her words as amusement sparkled in his eyes.

'No, we found other ways to spend the time, and the local tavernas met most of our remaining needs, as I intend they should now, certainly as far as I'm concerned; but you're free to make your own arrangements, naturally. If your memory needs refreshing as to how to get to the village or where the shops are...?' He paused delicately, dark eyebrows raised quizzically.

'Thank you, I'm sure it'll come back to me,' she told him stiffly.

'Good, I thought perhaps it might.' Satisfaction burred the timbre of his voice. 'In which case you won't need any advice from me. On most of the days, I'll be working in my own room, de-bugging the latest program we've produced, and I'll be responsible for my own meals. You can tell the children that I'll see them on the beach when I can find time. Does that suit you?'

'It sounds ideal.' Sapphira nodded. On the point of leaving the room she hesitated. 'Just how long do you envisage staying here?' she asked, with commendable coolness.

Beneath the intensity of his sombre gaze, her whole body seemed to tingle. 'Just as long as it's necessary.' The upward flare of his dark eyebrows presaged his curiosity. 'Why—do you have social engagements you may need to cancel?'

'No,' she said tersely. 'But I want to get on with my own life in my own way as soon as possible.'

As she walked from the room, her head held high, her mules clacking on the wooden floor, she thought she heard him laugh.

As each sun-filled day was followed by another, Sapphira found herself settling into a lazy routine of eating, sleeping, and relaxing with a book on the shady terrace overlooking the beach, sometimes joining Spiridoula on the beach as she supervised the twins playing together beneath the shade of a large sun umbrella.

The Greek girl was certainly an excellent employee, she now admitted, ashamed of her earlier unreasonable antipathy towards her. The children were obviously happy in her company, and she seemed to harbour no desire to leave them to seek her own amusement, although Sapphira had exhorted her on several occasions to take off whatever time she needed.

Ten days later, finishing a romantic novel with a sigh of satisfaction, Sapphira laid the book down on the terrace table and helped herself to a glass of iced lemonade from the prepared jug beside her. How peaceful it was, here in the open air, sheltered from the punishing rays of the sun by the spreading canopy of interlaced bamboo. It was Lorna who had supplied her with a dozen paperbacks, all of the same genre, all in English, as part of what she'd laughingly termed the 'therapeutic pack' she must take with her.

'Take them and enjoy them,' she'd told Sapphira dismissively. 'They'll help you to believe again in happy endings, despite traumatic intervals.'

'Escapism?' Sapphira had queried with a rueful smile.

'What's wrong with that?' Lorna had shot back. 'No one could accuse me of being sentimental, but I do happen to believe that the right mental attitude can work wonders. Think happy—be happy! The last thing you want at the moment, my dear, is to wallow in self-pity! So relax and believe!'

Lorna had certainly had a point, Sapphira admitted. She was finding the books compulsive reading, and was finishing each one with a feeling of deep contentment. It was pleasant to visualise other people surmounting their problems and achieving happy endings, even if she was to be denied one!

In fact she was feeling a lot better now than when she'd first arrived. Of course, being with the children had helped, along with the general lazy ambience of the island which had prevented her from thinking too much of the coming days. It was also true that Lorna's thoughtfulness was paying dividends. She looked down at her hands, recognising how greatly her skin had improved since she had been obediently following the instructions on the moisturising creams with which she'd been provided.

'Just because you don't love Thane any more, it's no excuse to give up loving yourself,' Lorna had lectured her. 'You have to make the best of yourself for your own sake, Sapphy. Pride, self-respect...to be confident you have to project self-confidence, and that means caring for yourself...'

Lorna had shown her kindness and understanding when she'd been so desperately in need of it, so the least she could do was to comply with her wishes, even to the extent of wearing the apricot satin negligé with which she'd been presented, although it was more suited to a Hollywood boudoir than a farmhouse on a remote Greek island!

Yet her friend had been right. Day by day Sapphira had both seen and felt an improvement in her appearance. She even suspected that she'd put on some badly needed weight: and she was becoming capable of more depth of feeling. The dreadful cold numbness which had held her in its thrall after she had heard the decision of the court to separate the twins seemed to be lifting, so that her responses to the sights and sounds around her had become sharpened, more appreciative...

Replacing the empty glass on the table, she rose to her feet to look out over the bay. It was late afternoon, and, as usual, Spiridoula was looking after the twins on the beach. Most afternoons they had the beach to themselves, tourists being few and far between, and the locals not wandering far from the town beach a fifteen-minute walk away. Today was different. Today Thane had joined them.

Instinctively, Sapphira's fingers tightened in her palms as she heard the laughter in his deep voice, and her eyes sought him out with an unwilling compulsion. He was emerging from the sea as her reluctant eyes lingered on him, dark bathing shorts concealing yet somehow augmenting his inherent masculinity, the powerful torso glistening with sea salt, the golden thighs and well-shaped calves with their light covering of hair striding through the light surf with the ease of a man who was master of his destiny.

Feeling her breath catch in her throat, Sapphira wondered momentarily at her own reaction. It was almost as if she were seeing him again for the first time, experiencing that glow of wonderment, a latent excitement that had fed its magic into every cell of her body. It had been his projection of total authority which had initially trapped, then annihilated her, Thane—lord, master...

Stop it! She had to crush this way of thinking. Months of separation had blessed her with immunity. How was it possible that her treacherous body had remembered its historical responses? The books. It had to be the books, she decided. Reading about other people's love affairs, however fictional, had stimulated the conditioned learning of her own body. Too late now to undo the mischief—but there was nothing that said she had to remain sitting there watching him, feeding her soul on his physical beauty. All she had to do was turn away and go upstairs to her bedroom.

She stayed where she was, hidden by the dark shadows cast by the canopy, as Thane walked easily towards the house. Reaching the garden shower, he stood beneath it, reaching one hand out to activate the spray. The water gushed out, streaming over his body, running in heavy rivulets over his shoulders and chest as he held his face up, eyes closed towards the sun.

Dear God, but he was magnificent! When his hands moved to the waistband of his shorts, and he eased the elastic outwards to allow the cooling, refreshing water to strike his naked skin and wash away the deposits of sand made by the movement of the sea, Sapphira gasped, empathetically sharing the shock of the cool spring water as it struck the most sensitive parts of his anatomy.

When he turned the shower off, reached for the towel he had left over the nearby wall and turned his narrowed eyes in her direction, Sapphira decided that she'd had enough. Shocked out of a long-existent lethargy, and beset with instinctive feelings she'd never wanted to feel again, she crept back into the house, running like a fugitive when she gained its sanctuary, until she was safely behind the closed door of her room, where she rested for a moment, feeling the heavy beating of her heart like a drum-roll against her ribs.

A cool shower would put matters in perspective, she decided, moving away, kicking off her sandals and pulling her dress over her head. Her fingers had already unfastened and discarded the light cotton bra she wore when her door resounded to a loud peremptory knock.

There was only one person who would knock like that! For a second, she even considered ignoring it. The knock came again, louder, if anything.

'Sapphira? I want to ask you something.'

She heard his impatience and quailed. There was no reason for her to be afraid of seeing him, she told herself firmly. Besides, all he had to do was push the door open. She found herself mildly surprised that he hadn't already resorted to that course of action—and if he had....

'Wait!' Panic sharpened the instruction as she reached for the nearest cover—the long apricot satin coat which added respectability to its accompanying nightdress. Thrusting her arms into it, she wrapped it round her half-naked body, firmly tying its sash. A quick glance in the mirror showed her a slender girl with the facial

bones of a 1960s magazine cover beauty, sharp yet delicate, a fragile frame for sensitive, compassionate eyes,
and a body adequately covered from neck to ankle.

It was only when she opened the door, and saw Thane
standing on the threshold, that she realised she'd expected
he would be in the state of undress she'd already observed. Her pulse quietened as she saw she had been
wrong.

'Can you spare me a few moments?' he asked, with
all the courtesy of a doorstep gospeller. His hair slicked
back, damp from the shower, his lean frame clothed in
a sleeveless, silver-grey stretch-cotton shirt which faith-
fully followed the tapering triangle of his torso over close-
fitting dark trousers, she realised, with a sinking heart,
that the impression he made was only marginally less
disturbing.

'Of course.' Disturbed because, for all her prep-
aration and the unexpected modesty of his attire, she
couldn't quell the rising unease which twisted her in-
sides, Sapphira echoed his politeness, stepping back to
allow him entry.

Seemingly in no great hurry, he halted, his eyes making
an unhurried passage over her face and dropping to
follow the lines of the satin coat with studied interest,
before he asked, 'Are you sleeping well, Sapphy?'

Uneasy beneath his close scrutiny, she could do no
more than nod, masking her agitation as he walked
further into the room to stop by the double bed, where
she had amused herself by laying out the apricot negligé
as if it were engaged in some sinuous dance.

Her breath caught in her throat, as, with sensitive
fingers, Thane touched the satin ribbon which sprung
in two tendrils from the low cut cleavage of silk.

'Do you have happy dreams—or do you find the absence of your new friend detracts from your rest?' Im-

possible not to be infuriated by the gleaming mockery
of his sage eyes.

With a *sang-froid* she was far from feeling, she
shrugged her shoulders in careless dismissal, choosing
deliberately to misunderstand his meaning. 'I sleep ex-
cellently, thank you. Ever since I moved in with Lorna,
the nights no longer hold any dread for me.'

Dark eyebrows winged momentarily upwards, but not
before she'd observed his jaw tighten in reaction to her
taunt. 'I'm delighted to hear your nervous system is fully
restored to its usual composed state.' His able fingers
caressed the silken material. 'But it was the absence of
your other friend to whom I was referring—the faithful
Michael.'

She wanted to laugh, because, although she liked
Michael and found him a comfortable companion,
Thane's insistence that he was, or could become, her
lover was ridiculous! Couldn't he see that he himself had
so drained her of passion that there was nothing left to
bestow on another man? Indignation quickly subdued
her amusement. She was tired of continually protesting
her lack of interest. Let him believe what he wanted to!

'That's hardly any business of yours, is it?' she responded coldly.

'If your behaviour brings discredit on our children, it
is!' came the quick riposte, the sharpness of anger thickening the consonants.

'How dare you?' Her temper rose to meet his own.
'You, of all people, are in no position to cast stones!'

For a moment, his brow creased in puzzlement, then
the corners of his mobile mouth twitched as the allusion
registered. 'Ah, yes, I understand. "Let him who is
without sin," eh?' His smile was thoughtful, and instinctively she knew that he wasn't going to go through
the farce of denying her allegation. It was something he

had long ceased to do. 'It would be a great pity, though, if you chose to jump out of the frying pan down the drain!'

This time she did laugh, feeling amusement bubbling upwards from her tense diaphragm and tickling her throat until she was able to expel it. The disparaging cast of Thane's distinctive features did nothing to curb her hilarity.

'I'm sorry, Thane,' she apologised, without sincerity. 'Your English is magnificent, but the saying is "out of the frying pan into the fire"!'

'In this case, my version is more illustrative, I think,' he returned silkily, in no way abashed by her correction. 'The man is a preparer of food, a washer of dishes—a drain seems an apposite comparison to me.'

'And you are an intellectual snob!' she flared back. 'Michael is a trained and creative chef who is also a part-owner of the restaurant in which he works. And even if he earned his living washing dishes, do you think it would make any difference to me?'

His shrug was barely perceptible. 'A man is partly what he does!'

'Which makes *you* an unemotional, logical processor of data, unable to make subjective judgements based on pity, compassion or understanding! Hard! Cruel! And unimaginative!' Sapphira's hand flew to her throat in despair as she spat out the last word. What was she doing? Dear God, she'd thought the fighting was behind her and now she'd allowed Thane to provoke her...

'Your reading of my character is excellent.' He gave her a slight bow, causing her to remove her gaze from his derisive face. 'But there are many elements which combine in the making of a man. It is possible you have not discovered them all.'

'Or that I shouldn't want to,' she murmured. 'Was your concern about my sleeping habits the only reason you came here?'

'Your sleeping habits will always concern me, Sapphy *mou*.' His eyes rested on her with cool speculation as he deliberately misconstrued her meaning. 'But there was another reason. I've reserved a table for the two of us tonight at one of the tavernas. I'll pick you up at eight this evening.'

He was unbelievable! Sapphira sucked in a deep breath, wondering how best to turn down his autocratic decision with dignity.

'It's very kind of you,' she said coldly, 'but I've already prepared a cold chicken salad for all of us tonight.'

'All of us?' he queried sardonically. 'I'm afraid I must have mislaid your invitation.'

'All of us—except you,' she responded between her teeth, 'since you said you'd be responsible for your own sustenance!'

'Afraid to trust yourself alone with me, Sapphy?' He turned to regard her, with a quizzical lift of one eyebrow. 'What on earth do you suppose I would do to you in full view of several dining Greeks, even if I weren't officially barred from molesting you?'

She knew that smile. There was nothing humorous about it. It was a warning of stormy seas ahead, and every cell in her body went on alert at the sight of it.

'There are other forms of abuse apart from the physical,' she returned tartly, her body warming at her own temerity. 'I've no wish to spend the evening being insulted!'

'You really suppose that's my purpose?' He managed to look magnificently hurt. 'I can assure you, my motives are at the same time both more pleasant and more prosaic. I thought we could take the opportunity of being

comparatively alone to discuss where you'll live when
we return to Kethina. Even as a temporary measure, your
present accommodation is far from satisfactory. Of
course——' he shrugged his shoulders '—if you would
prefer that we discuss the matter here and now...' He
studied the rise and fall of the satin covering her breasts
with steady-eyed interest, as she became aware of the
pointed thrust of her nipples against its soft covering.

CHAPTER FIVE

'No!' SHE answered too quickly, and saw his tigerish smile once more, as her brain worked at lightning speed. He was right. They *would* have to discuss her future habitation, and a quiet taverna would be as good a place as any. A pang of unhappiness squeezed her heart. Despite everything, it seemed like robbery on her part to take so much of Thane's hard-earned estate. On the other hand, she couldn't take advantage of Lorna's hospitality for much longer. Hopefully, there could be a compromise where she could accept less than he had offered to the court.

'Well?' Thane prompted her gently. 'We could make it a celebration dinner at the same time.'

'Toast the end of our marriage, you mean?' For some unaccountable reason it was as if he'd thrust a sword through her heart. Yet, in truth, the marriage had been dead or dying for years...

'That would be a false premise, *agape mou*——' the cynical endearment curled off his tongue like the hiss of a snake '—since—however much you desired it otherwise—you are still my wife.'

'In nothing but name!'

'But still my wife. Still the mother of my children, *ne*, Sapphira?' He didn't wait for her answer. 'That, perhaps, might be worth celebrating; but no, the celebration I had in mind was your birthday.'

'My... birthday?' She'd rarely felt so stupid before. Forgetting her own birthday! Yet there was some excuse. Apart from the trauma of recent events, birthdays were not much acknowledged in Greece, celebrations being reserved for one's name day instead.

As far as she knew there was no Saint Sapphira, her namesake probably having been condemned to hellfire for supporting her husband's lie, she contemplated a little sourly. Therefore, she'd retained her birthday as a special occasion—and Thane had remembered it.

'I'd quite forgotten,' she confessed, a trifle shamefacedly.

'Easy enough to do.' He was quick to support her. 'Especially as your birthday cards from England will be waiting for you in Kethina. Having deprived you of the pleasure of opening them on the day, the least I can do in reparation is offer you a good meal with good wine. Unless, of course, you find my company totally repulsive?'

Impossible to live with—but repulsive? Never. It was *he* who found *her* repulsive, wasn't it? The memory of the last time she had shared his bed returned to haunt her. Too wounded to even attempt a lie to save face, she made a small gesture with her hands, and begged the question.

'We do need to talk about the future, I suppose.'

'Then eight o'clock it is.' He sounded pleased and sure of himself, as well he might. 'I've already told Spiridoula we shan't be back till late.'

As soon as he had left the room, Sapphira took her shower, wishing she could rinse away the unsettling effect he still exerted over her as easily as she could eliminate the exotically perfumed body shampoo which had been yet another ingredient of Lorna's gift.

There had been a cruel undertone to Thane's apparently courteous enquiry about the comfort of her sleep, as if he guessed that sleeping once more in the bed where they'd both found such exquisite fulfilment augmented the emotional emptiness which was her everyday companion. The price she was being asked to pay for these last few days, which mocked the family closeness she had longed for, was a bitter one!

Stepping from the shower and reaching for the towel, she sighed, a deep expelling of breath which removed some of the tension from her muscles. How excited she'd been when she had learned she was expecting twins, and how that joy had been eroded by ill-health and the anxiety following their delivery by Caesarian section, followed by their confinement in the intensive care unit.

She'd returned home to find that Thane had appointed Spiridoula as a nursery-maid. Fraught with apprehension about the twins' survival and her own total lack of the elation she'd anticipated, she'd resented the young Greek girl's presence as an indictment of her own inadequacies, particularly since, despite total commitment to the idea, she'd been quite unable to feed the babies herself.

Frantically, she'd demanded that the children share the master bedroom with their parents, so that she could give them twenty-four-hour supervision.

Thane had shocked her with his adamant refusal. 'For God's sake, Sapphy, don't you realise that I'm still slaving to get the consultancy firmly established? It's a developing industry, and we have to stay in the forefront or perish! I don't need a lot of sleep, but what I do get must be uninterrupted, or we'll all end up bankrupt!'

'You're uncaring and selfish!' she'd flared back. 'They're your children—your obligation. As it is, they hardly ever see you!'

'Because I'm fulfilling that obligation by earning the money to support them!'

Was it possible to love and hate a man at the same time? Seeing no compassion in his hard face, she had thought it must be.

'Be reasonable, Sapphy. We both love them, but your love is obsessive!' He'd added, after a pause, his tone more gentle, 'You already spend every waking moment with them, and Spiridoula sleeps in the adjoining room with the door open. If they are in any way distressed she knows she can summon us immediately.'

She'd refused to be placated.

'If that's how you feel, then I'll have a bed put into the nursery and sleep there!'

If he'd forbidden it, perhaps their relationship wouldn't have deteriorated so swiftly. But he hadn't, and she'd gone ahead with her plans. Afterwards, the arguments between them had grown worse, often starting over something trivial and growing into a torrent of exchanged verbal abuse. Because of their lack of tactile communion, there had been no kiss of forgiveness or caress of understanding. She'd felt drained of vitality, seeing her life in monochrome values, hating what she'd become, but unable to find either the energy or willpower to alter it.

Thoughtfully, Sapphira reached for the aerosol of body-foam, and began to smooth the soft cream into her skin, healthily glowing now from its careful exposure to the sun.

No one had been more conscious than she of how awful she had looked, or more hurt, when Thane had started escorting Angelia Andronicos to the social functions she had refused to attend with him.

The twins had been eighteen months old when she'd confronted him with this act of treachery.

He'd been in the process of fastening the cuffs of his shirt with gold links, when she'd stormed into the bedroom she no longer shared with him, accusing him of demeaning her. 'If you must go, why don't you go alone?' she'd demanded.

His cold appraisal of her contentious face had made the pulse at the base of her throat hammer.

'Would you deprive me of all congenial company?' he'd asked with icy control. 'Angelia, as you know, is the sister of my co-director, as well as secretary of the company. She's not only beautiful and *simpatica*, but a good friend, whose company I value.'

Even now, after all that time, she could remember how the level declaration had wounded her, piercing her thin skin with the ease of a needle stabbing silk.

'In bed, as well as out of it?' she'd sneered and watched his jaw grow tight with barely controlled fury.

'Since you no longer wish to share my bed yourself, your interest in who does is impertinent. I have no intention of supplying you with a list!'

A list! She'd blanched at the venom in his deep voice.

'However,' he'd continued with a softness more frightening that if he'd shouted at her, 'you will not voice that allegation about Angelia again, or I'll see you regret it. Since you are no longer desirous of accompanying me on an occasion such as tonight's, or suitable to do so, you will not malign the woman who has stepped into your shoes. Is that understood?'

For answer, she had stared wildly round the room, then, grabbing a digital alarm clock from the bedhead, she'd flung it straight at his face. He had moved from its path, but not before an edge had drawn blood from his eyebrow. Terrified and shamed by her action, she had fled from the room, but at the time it had been the only way she had been able to express her frustration at the heavy depression which had become her daily com-

panion, ruling her life and destroying the pride she'd
once had in herself and her appearance.

Thane hadn't returned that night and she'd sat alone
in the silent sitting-room, hugging a Metaxa to herself
with a shaking hand, homesick for the lost companionship of Abby and David and her parents. Thane had
never loved her. At last, she had been prepared to admit
the truth. Victim of her immature provocation and his
own sensual nature, he'd married her out of a sense of
honour because he'd taken her virginity—and been
caught in the process.

Satisfied that every inch of her skin was soft and
supple from the application of the gently perfumed foam,
Sapphira wandered now out into the bedroom and selected a delicate body-shaper of silk and lace as an under-
garment to the cotton dress she'd already decided to wear.

How astounded and thrilled she'd been when, less than
a week after that violent bitter encounter with Thane,
Abby had arrived on the doorstep, complete with a large
suitcase, announcing that she'd come to spend part of
her long summer holiday with them—if she was
welcome!

At the time she'd doubted that Thane would willingly
accept a member of her family into their divided
household, but she'd been wrong. Her husband had welcomed her sister with open arms—quite literally.

Damn! She must stop torturing herself like this. If
there'd been any chance along the way of saving her
marriage, it was long since past. If Thane hadn't found
consolation with her sister, it would have been with
someone else. Abby had long since returned to England,
but wasn't Angelia Andronicos still a constant and intimate presence in his life? Somehow, she would force
herself to cope with the results of the tragic mistake they
had both made.

* * *

She was taking a final look at the sleeping twins before going downstairs to meet Thane, when she heard him enter the room.

'Beautiful, aren't they?' he breathed softly, placing a gentle arm around her shoulders, inviting her to enjoy his pleasure. He'd changed his cotton shirt for an open-necked soft green sports shirt, and his hair had been carefully groomed to flatter his broad forehead and re-markable eyes.

'Yes.' A quick glance at his face showed her the pride and love there. How she could possibly have once sus-pected that he had no feeling for them?

A fleeting sadness was mirrored in his eyes as he turned and regarded her, holding her gaze with a dark force which made it impossible for her to turn away. 'Tell me, Sapphy—was all your suffering worth it?'

Toxaemia, the Caesarian, the weeks of endless torment when she'd truly believed they wouldn't survive... But there was no doubt in her mind. 'Of course,' she said simply, and flinched as his hand tightened against her arm.

'Ready then?' Sensitive to her response, he released his hold.

'Certainly.'

She'd selected a fuchsia and grey bold print cotton dress from the wardrobe. With a V-neck, capped and split sleeves, and full skirt cinched by a matching fuchsia belt, it was a flattering style, particularly when teamed with slender-heeled grey sandals, and she couldn't help but be aware how intently his eyes dwelt on her as she descended the stairs.

She waited tensely for some comment, a sarcastic remark, perhaps, about her sudden awakening of interest in presenting herself groomed for the occasion. But, apart from what she could only take to be a slight glimmer of appreciation in his speculative eyes as he opened the front door and allowed her to precede him, he made no reference either to her dress or her make-up. At least he hadn't criticised her, she thought triumphantly, suppressing a pang of conscience which suggested that, on this occasion, he had no grounds for criticism!

'I thought we'd go to Vassili's,' he informed her pleasantly, 'It's unlikely to be crowded but, in any case, I've asked Vassili to reserve a table for us, overlooking the sea. Perhaps you've already discovered his taverna?'

'No.' She shook her head, tensing as he placed a competent hand beneath her elbow, but not recoiling from it.

'Ah.' He sounded pleased. 'You'll find his place is a cut above the other tavernas—he's got a few specialities you won't find outside a four-star restaurant.'

'I'm looking forward to it,' she returned politely, as they started out on the short walk to where Vassili's taverna was built, on a jutting area of cliff immediately over the far side of the horseshoe bay. With every table laid with a linen cloth, silver, glasses and a tiny vase of fresh flowers, it was certainly different from its competitors, she observed with interest, as the proprietor came to greet them.

'Vassili has only been here just over a year but he has a very select and discriminating clientele,' Thane said as he registered her surprise, 'especially among the yachting fraternity. You'd be surprised how far people are prepared to travel to sample Vassili's steak Diane or lobster thermidor.'

Nearly two hours later, no amount of sea miles travelled would have surprised her. Having enjoyed a meal of prawns deep fried in cheese batter, followed by pepper steak with a Greek salad, and crêpes Suzette *flambéd* at

the table before her, the whole accompanied by a light
dry crisp Cretan wine, suitably chilled, her sense of
disbelief had become suspended.

She'd anticipated feeling awkward in Thane's critical
presence, wondering if, with her tummy knotted with
tension, she'd be able to do justice to the meal. At least,
she had comforted herself, with the taverna well-
patronised, their discussion about their future shouldn't
deteriorate into the kind of slanging match which had
characterised their recent communications!

When it became clear that whatever he had to say was
going to have to wait until the arrival of coffee and
liqueurs, she began to relax. The atmosphere was perfect,
she admitted: the breeze warm and gentle, the sky clear,
with a half-moon bright on the horizon, casting a
pathway of silver across the glistening darkness of the
sea, and, in the background, softly muted mood music.
A setting wasted on ex-lovers, she decided, conscious of
a twinge of pain twisting inside her. Although, from the
casual way in which Thane appeared to be enjoying his
meal, his fine body at ease, his appetite in no way im-
paired, it was obvious that he didn't see the irony of the
surroundings.

'Oh!' She gave a little gasp as the overhead lights suddenly went out, leaving the tables illuminated only by
their own dim lamps, her gaze going automatically to
the location of the kitchen as a ripple of applause
sounded round the tables nearest to it.

It was Vassili himself who appeared, triumphantly
bearing a tall glass piled up with fruit and ice-cream,
and copiously decorated with indoor fireworks which
spluttered and flared as he bore it towards her.

'Congratulations, *kyria*!' He placed the exploding
confection before her. 'May you live to be a hundred.
This is with the compliments of the management.'

'Oh, but I can't...' Horrified by the size of the offering, she began to protest, her words faltering to a stop as the lights resumed their former brilliance and she could see the disappointment lengthening Vassili's rotund face. 'I mean—what a marvellous surprise!' she amended hastily. 'I can't thank you enough—it looks...' words almost failed her '...magnificent!' she finished, a trifle weakly.

'Four kinds of ice-cream, black cherries, melon and plenty of advocaat!' the proprietor told her cheerfully. 'It is quite renowned.'

'I'm sure it must be.' She smiled at Vassili, then, catching Thane's obvious amusement, added sweetly, 'Perhaps we could have another spoon, Vassili? Such a creation deserves to be shared.'

'At once, *kyria*.' He snapped his fingers and gave his order to a passing waiter, laying down the resultant spoon in front of Thane. 'Enjoy your celebration.'

'Touché.' The glimmer of rueful admiration in Thane's long-lashed eyes gave her grudging approval. 'You know I'm no lover of ice-cream.'

'And *you* know I don't have a large appetite!' she defended herself. 'It's your fault he knows about my birthday—no one else could possibly have told him!'

He shrugged his shoulders laconically. 'I may have mentioned it when I asked for this table,' he admitted. 'I thought it would get us preferential treatment. I must admit, I'd forgotten his rather childish way of celebrating anniversaries among his guests.'

'Actually, I think it's rather charming—only he should have sprung the surprise before I ordered a dessert!'

'And lose the profit on his crêpes Suzettes?' Dark eyebrows rose in mockery. 'Ah, well, we mustn't offend him, so I guess I will have to help you out.' He dug his spoon deep into the colourful mixture, transferring its contents to his mouth. 'It really is quite delicious.' He gave his verdict after a few moments' deliberation. 'Try some.' Digging his spoon in deeply, he offered it across the table.

She hesitated marginally, aware of the challenge in his insouciant gesture. Yet, what harm could there be in allowing him this small victory? Obediently she opened her mouth, closing her eyes as she felt the bowl of the spoon on her tongue. 'Delicious,' she murmured when she'd got her breath back, and saw from the satisfied glitter of his laughing eyes that he was well satisfied with her response.

Between them, they cleared the glass, taking their time and savouring the rich flavours.

'Quite a time since we last shared a loving cup, *ne*, Sapphira?' Carefully, Thane placed his spoon on the plate at the base of the glass. 'And probably the last we ever shall, which reminds me, I have something for you.'

Quickly, she looked away from his evaluating gaze, blinking her eyes in an effort to brush away the quick start of tears his words had engendered. There had been wonderful days in the past . . . if only he had loved her as much as she had loved him . . .

'Sapphira . . .'

'Yes?'

'Just a little gift to celebrate your birthday, and to say *"sto kalo."*' He offered her a small box.

The phrase he'd chosen had a very definite meaning in Greek. Used mainly to people who were about to go from one's life for ever, it had the meaning of "wherever you go, may you encounter something good". To refuse to take it would be churlish and offensive, but somewhere in the back of her mind she remembered the phrase, "I fear the Greeks even when they bear gifts". What new humiliation might he have in store for her?

'Take it, Sapphira!' It was as if he'd read her thoughts, his voice deepening with quiet intensity.

Silently, she accepted the box, breaking the seal, and lifting the lid to expose a beautifully made egg of pale blue Parian porcelain, bearing a design, in white relief, of a winged Cupid, bow in hand, quiver on his back.

It was a collector's piece. When she'd been fifteen she'd chanced across a similar piece in Limoges porcelain and had spent every penny of her hard-earned savings to purchase it. It was still one of her most treasured possessions—and he had known it.

'It's exquisite!' She let it lie in her palm, feeling its weight, loving its beauty, and was filled with a deep, aching sadness she didn't attempt to analyse.

'In my country, an egg symbolises a new life—a new beginning. I'm gratified that it pleases you.' Raising an imperative finger, he signalled the waiter to refill the brandy glass which stood on the table before him. 'And now, to business, Sapphira.' He waited until the bowl of the glass reflected the rich golden spirit and the waiter had moved away, before breaking the sudden aura of tension which had deepened between them. 'I've decided to make a complete break with the past. I intend to sell the Villa Andromeda.'

'Oh, no!' Too late to prevent the agonised protest escaping her lips, Sapphira instantly covered them with the fingers of her left hand. It was the last thing she'd been prepared for. Losing her own occupation of it had been one thing, but the prospect of its being sold chilled her like a blast of cold air. She'd imagined the twins growing up there, enjoying the spacious rooms, playing in the extensive gardens she'd taken so much joy in designing and planting under Thane's indulgent eye. Originally designed for a wealthy American, it had come on the market shortly after their marriage, when the original owner had had to return to the States to take over family responsibilities there. She'd fallen in love with it at first sight, and during the first year of her marriage had delighted in putting her own personal stamp on it. 'Do you really have to?'

'Since I have to provide you with a separate residence, there's really very little option, I'm afraid. Besides, it's only breeze blocks and cement made into an architect's concept of gracious living. Once, I might have considered it a seventh heaven—but that was an illusion we both suffered from at the time, *ne*?'

'But I need very little!' In her anguish she leant across the table towards him. 'I can manage in a couple of rooms now I've given up permanent custody of Victoria. Give me a little time and I'll get a job to support myself...'

'You're talking nonsense.' His jaw tightened ominously. 'Quite apart from your rights in the matter, you are entitled to have both children to stay with you from time to time. For their sakes, you'll have to live in acceptable surroundings.'

'I hadn't thought that far ahead...' she admitted, frankly. All she'd wanted to do was to get away from the man whose unyielding presence in her life tormented her beyond endurance.

'It may take a little time to find a buyer,' he was continuing evenly. 'After all, it's a large property, and the housing market here is rather different from that in the UK. In the meantime, I have an agent looking for suitable temporary accommodation for you. With any luck, when we return to Kethina, he will have found it.'

'You shouldn't have gone to so much trouble—Lorna is quite happy for me to share her apartment until...'

'But *I'm* not!' He interrupted savagely. 'That *maliosa* put a spell on you in that hospital. She took advantage of your refusal to see me to poison your mind, and she's been doing it ever since!'

He couldn't have been more wrong, but nothing she could say in Lorna's defence would persuade him otherwise. He didn't have to love her to be jealous of anyone whom he presumed to hold influence over her. She recognised the instinct of the wild stallion to exercise total dominance over every member of his herd. The fact that she had found a way to leave that herd counted not one iota with him!

Instead, she countered coldly, 'And you think my mind wasn't already poisoned after I found you and my sister locked in each other's arms?'

He said something brief and forceful in his own language, which had heads at other tables turning to regard him with a mixture of shock and amusement, as he pushed his chair back and rose to his feet.

'I think it's time we left.' He thrust his hand into his trouser pocket to pull forth a handful of drachma notes, giving her no option but to join him as he turned to leave.

Outside, her high heels caught on a stone and she stumbled, saved from falling only by Thane's steadying hold on her bare arm. Instinctively, she shrank from his warm touch on her skin, cursing herself silently for the effect he still had on her, her despair deepening as she realised he hadn't been impervious to her reaction.

'Theos mou!' he growled, his hand tightening on her trembling flesh. 'Must you react to me as if I were about to rape you?'

Alone in the dark street, she fought to control the mixture of fear and anger which sent the blood pulsing through her veins, the silence broken only by the monotonous signal of the cicadas, as a light breeze moved her skirt against her legs and stirred the pale halo of her hair.

'I prefer not to be touched,' she muttered unhappily, through lips still warmed by the liqueur she had consumed.

'By me, you mean,' he riposted grimly, pulling her closer, taking no heed of her sharp protest. 'Why is it that I still have this feeling you're preparing to kick over the traces? Desert our children, turn your back on this part of your life completely?' His voice, low and husky, so close to her ear, reminded her forcefully of earlier, happier times, so that she was shamed to experience a long-dormant thrill of heat flooding through her sensitive skin. 'By God, I wish I had the right to beat the truth out of you!'

'No!' Her half-strangulated denial didn't seem to impress him. 'I've never lied to you!'

Held so close to his heart, she found the control of which she'd been so proud disintegrating. The blood seemed to be singing in her ears as her nerves clamoured in pitiful disorganisation. 'In any case, what business would it be of yours? You no longer have any control over me!'

'I'm not sure either of us really believes that,' he told her softly, his fingers moving sensuously against her upper arm, as a dark magnetic current seemed to enfold them.

She stared at him, her luminous eyes betraying her panic, aware of the tension which possessed his lean body. He had no right to disturb her like this. Her breath sharpened in her throat as she tried to free herself.

Impervious to her weak struggle, he caressed her softly with his voice. 'Shall we put it to the test?'

Sliding his hands up under her shoulders, he possessed her mouth with his own. The kiss was unrelentingly hard against her tender lips, awakening a long-dormant heat in her loins. When he finally withdrew, he still pinioned her with icily brilliant eyes, devoid of either sympathy or regret for the degradation he had forced on her. 'And if you're thinking of turning me in to the police for breach of our agreement, then be warned—I shall plead provocation!'

She had invited nothing, certainly not this crude attempt to humiliate her; but dignity lay in refusing to fight him.

'Is there anything else you wish to discuss?' she asked calmly, through lips which still throbbed. 'Because, if not, I should like to get back.'

'By all means.' The words pleased her, but she didn't care for the silkiness of his expression as his eyes lingered on her flushed face. 'I've achieved what I came here to do, so there's nothing else to be gained by remaining on the island. I'd be grateful if you would instruct Spiridoula to be ready to leave for the mainland by midday tomorrow.'

CHAPTER SIX

'THANK you, Michael. It's been a lovely evening.' Accepting her escort's hand, Sapphira eased herself from the grey Peugeot, alighting to stand in the small courtyard in front of the small block of apartments which contained the new flat Thane's agent had found for her.

The words were trite enough, but none the less honest for that. The drive into Athens, the leisurely stroll through the shopping area, followed by a relaxed dinner in an open-air restaurant, had served to relieve her mind temporarily from the weight of misery which had continued to subdue her since her return from Konstantinos, and she was grateful that Michael had suggested they spend one of his rare days off together.

For the five days since her return, in accordance with the visiting rights decreed by the court under the original settlement, she hadn't seen the twins. It had been an agonising time for her, in which she had lectured herself in the darkest hours before the dawn, when sleep eluded her, that the children's welfare had to take precedence over her own fragile emotions.

'We must do it again, Sapphira.' Lorna's brother placed a casual arm across her shoulders, guiding her through the stone archway which led to the inner courtyard. 'I would have suggested it before, but while you were still married it could have led to hurtful speculation.'

Not to mention a hurtful confrontation with her husband if Thane had found out! Sapphira thought ruefully, but contented herself by saying, 'I still am married, Michael.'

'But it's not the same!' he returned angrily. 'Just because that swine wouldn't give you your total freedom, it doesn't mean you still have to consider his feelings. He's just being pig-headed! Besides, what's to stop you from living your own life? It's not as if he can take the children from you, since you've already given them up!'

'I haven't given them up!' Forcefully she denied it. 'All I've done is waive my claim voluntarily so that the twins can share the same household. I could change my mind at any time, I'm sure of it, provided I don't give Thane any reason to argue that I've become unfit to look after Victoria. Can't you see the difference?' She looked at him beseechingly. 'I can bear to live apart from them because I know it's of my own choosing, but if Thane thought he had grounds to get the order changed officially...that would be unendurable!'

'Sapphy, you're shaking.' His voice gentled. 'I'm sorry. I didn't mean to upset you, but I can't help wondering why you didn't try to prove that Thane was an unfit father.'

'Because—because I assumed that I, as the mother, would automatically get custody; in any case, I couldn't prove his infidelity, and even if I had been able to, I'm not sure it would have gone against him. I get the feeling that Greek men expect, and are expected, to be unfaithful to their wives almost as a proof of their virility!'

It wasn't the entire truth. The thought of accusing Thane in public had revolted her. Besides, he'd never argued that she might be an unfit mother, although the way she'd behaved in the grey days following the twins' birth and when she'd found him in Abby's arms could have been used by a lesser man to cast doubts on her mental stability. His restraint in that respect had earned him a big plus on the credit side of the mental ledger that balanced the rise and fall of her marriage; but then he'd known so much more about Greek justice than she had...

'I guess you could argue that the majority of men feel the same way.' Michael's pleasant face broke into a grin, as he interrupted her train of thought. 'Not that I'm including myself in their number.'

'You're a nice guy, Michael.' Sapphira patted the hand which rested on her shoulder. 'I'm surprised that some lovely Greek *thespinis* hasn't fallen for you.'

'Fat chance of that!' He laughed. 'You know as well as, if not better than, I do, that, while the Greek family clan may open their doors to a foreign bride on the assumption that she will be assimilated into their culture by her dominant husband, no such concession is offered to a foreign male trying to steal one of their daughters! Besides,' he added softly, gently squeezing her shoulder, 'I'm not in the market for romance. I've already found the woman I want.'

'Michael—no! Please don't!' She raised fearful eyes to stare into his serious face as they halted beside the communal entrance to the apartment block. 'I don't know what I should have done without you and Lorna, and I do regard both of you as my dearest friends— but—I'm not ready for any other kind of liaison.'

'But in time you will be.' He spoke confidently—a well-built young man in his late twenties whom many girls would have been delighted to acknowledge as a prospective lover. 'In fact, I was hoping that, now you've moved out of Lorna's place and got a flat of your own...' He paused delicately.

Ruefully, Sapphira shook her head. 'Even if I wanted to kick over the traces, it isn't as easy as that. I can't risk being labelled a scarlet woman.' Her warm mouth twisted into a wry smile.

'But if it weren't for the children?' he persisted.

'No; it's not what I want, Michael—please believe me.' Her voice broke in anguish. 'In fact, I think it would be better if we didn't see each other alone again.' She glanced away, unable to bear the hurt on his face. 'I'll have to go in now. I'm truly dreadfully tired.'

She took a pace backwards, but Michael was too quick for her, taking her by surprise, entwining his fingers in her flyaway hair, drawing her head towards his own, branding her mouth with an angry, passionate kiss.

'Damn Thanos Stavrolakes!' he cursed as he released her, shaken and saddened by the unexpected, powerful assault. 'Damn him to hell for the tyrant that he is! He's branded you with his mark as surely as if he'd taken a hot iron to you! Have it your own way, Sapphy. At least I'm a man who can accept "no" for an answer; but just remember, if you ever need me—you know where to find me!'

She watched him turn on his heel and walk with hunched shoulders towards his car. She'd never seen him so enraged, but then hadn't she always been a bad judge of men's characters? Sadly, she touched the bruised skin of her mouth. Fool that she was, she'd never suspected the depths of feeling to which he'd admitted. If frustration was going to bring out the beast in Michael, then her decision not to see him again had been a wise one, for both their sakes. She sighed. Nevertheless, she had engineered yet another gap in the fabric of her own life.

Putting her key in the lock, she turned it, pushing the door open, then freezing with fear as she saw a soft triangle of light glowing through the half-open door of her living-room. Swallowing her panic, she waited for her unsettled pulse to steady. The explanation was simple:

she'd obviously forgotten to reverse the switch before she'd left. Now that she was destined to live alone, she would have to keep a curb on her imagination.

With a resolute hand, she pushed the door to its full extreme, stifling a scream as a tall familiar figure came towards her.

'Where the hell have you been to this hour of the night?' Thane demanded imperiously.

'Out,' Sapphira returned, daring his anger, as she fought to control the aftermath of the shock she'd received. 'And what the hell are you doing, breaking in here?'

'Hardly breaking in, *agape mou*.' She flinched at the contempt in the endearment. 'Since I'm paying for this place, you'd expect me to have a key to it, wouldn't you?'

'But not to use it uninvited!' She was trembling. In the savage mood he was in she could hardly expect to win any argument against him, but some devil inside her forced her to confront him. 'Why have you come here, Thane?' she blazed at him fiercely.

The outline of his jaw was steely, the gleam in his eyes foreboding.

'To take you back to the Villa Andromeda.'

'What? You must be joking?' Image and reality merged as his tall figure seemed to blur. For one wild, impossible second she hallucinated that he had come to reclaim her as his wife, his love—the woman he couldn't live without—then the vision faded, and she saw from his thunderous expression that the truth must be very different.

'I wish I were!' he told her bitterly. 'Believe me, my errand isn't on my own behalf. These past few days have been amongst the most peaceful I've enjoyed since you set foot in Greece.'

His scorn was like a smack in the face, but she took it bravely, refusing to flinch before the cruelty of his stony gaze. 'Then why should you wish to prejudice that happy state of events?'

'Stephanos has had an accident.'

Afterwards she was to wonder if the bald statement had been to punish her; if so, he must have been very pleased at the result of his bombshell.

'Oh, my God! What's happened? Where is he?' In her anguish she grabbed hold of Thane's upper arms, ironically unaware that she was imitating a stance he had often taken with her. Her agitation removed all caution from her actions as, thumbs digging into his flesh, she attempted to shake an answer out of him. 'Is he dead?'

'Of course not. He's not even badly hurt.' The coolness of his reply went a long way to calming her as she fought the waves of nausea washing over her. 'A couple of days ago I had a swing installed in the garden,' he continued grimly. 'I thought it might prove a distraction for them. Instead of sitting strapped into the seat, as he's been told to do, our son decided to stand on it while Spiridoula was attending to Victoria. The result was inevitable. He fell off.'

'Is he concussed? Has he broken anything?' The questions came tumbling out as Sapphy clutched at him for support.

'Stop it, Sapphy!' For the first time, she sensed a note of compassion in Thane's deep voice as he took her hands away from his body, clasping them between his own strong palms. 'Calm down, and listen to me. It was more shock and fear of being punished for disobedience that upset him, but, naturally, I took him to the hospital and had him X-rayed. There's nothing wrong that nature won't heal in a few days except...'

'Except?' she prompted, anxiously.

Thane shrugged. 'Except he wants his mother. He knows he won't be seeing you every day, but he refuses to understand why you can't go to him when he's been hurt. He thinks he's being punished because he did something wrong, and he keeps saying he's sorry and asking when you'll forgive him.'

'I'll come at once.' Tears were welling over her lower lids, dripping down her face. She wiped them clear with the back of her hand, allowing him to guide her downstairs and to his car. Strange, she thought, that she hadn't noticed its sleek lines when she'd stood in the courtyard only minutes earlier, but then she'd been too occupied in refusing Michael's attentions.

Allowing Thane to assist her into the front passenger seat, she heard once more Michael's accusation against her estranged husband of tyranny ringing in her memory. It wasn't a title with which she would disagree, she thought bleakly. Her brain filled with concern for her son; just one tiny corner remained loyal to the past. Thane, lord, liege, master...

Minutes later, Spiridoula opened the front door before Thane could turn his key in the lock.

'He's sleeping now—both of them are.' Her wide smile was for Sapphira. 'He will be all right now you are here—you will see!'

'I must go up and see him.' Sapphira didn't wait to hear Thane's grunt of agreement or see Spiridoula's satisfied nod of approval. She was taking the stairs two at a time, her breath shallow with unspoken concern, clenching her teeth with resolve as she opened the door to the nursery, uncertain, despite Thane's assurances, what sight would meet her eyes.

Both children slept peacefully, their single beds separated by a table on which glowed a dim light.

'Oh, Stephanos, oh, baby!' she murmured, dropping down on her knees beside the little boy, touching his cool forehead with the tips of her fingers as if she could impart some message of comfort through the soft skin without waking him. 'Mummy's here, sweetheart.'

Carefully she lifted the single sheet which covered him to reveal the light cotton pyjamas he wore, her anxious eyes searching the small amount of revealed skin for signs of injury, and finding none. She hesitated, wanting for her own selfish sake to awaken him, to feel his clinging arms round her neck, while she assured herself that he wasn't badly hurt.

'Leave him, Sapphy. Let him sleep.' The curt, low-voiced order had her swinging round to see Thane watching her, his expression withdrawn, as if she were some interfering stranger. Pain twisted in her heart. He hadn't wanted her here. If Stephanos had found sleep earlier she would have been no wiser about the incident.

'I guess you're right.' It was incredibly difficult to relinquish her maternal urge, but it was pointless to disturb the child now he'd finally found rest. With a sigh she replaced the sheet, leaning forward to place a light kiss on the soft cheek, before turning to the other bed to give Victoria a similar salutation.

She rose to her feet, stumbling a little, the joint result of tiredness and shock, she supposed, as she met Thane's steady appraisal.

'Well, it seems I'm not indispensable, after all!' She tried to make a joke of it, but to her horror two tears escaped from her welling eyes to drip remorselessly down her cheeks. Stoically she ignored them. 'I'll phone you in the morning and see how he is, if that's all right?' She didn't wait for his answer, knowing he wouldn't begrudge her that. 'And now, if you could get a taxi for me I'd be more than grateful.'

'How much more, Sapphy?' He was watching her carefully, his face devoid of all expression. 'Enough to say goodbye to me as passionately as you did to your escort this evening?'

'You were spying on us!' Her voice rose in indignation as colour mantled her cheeks.

'Hush!' Thane led her forcefully from the nursery, closing the door behind them. 'The children have heard enough of our quarrels to last them a lifetime—for mercy's sake, let them sleep in peace.' He pushed her gently towards the stairs. 'We can finish this conversation downstairs, if that's what you want.'

'No, no, I just want to get back to my flat,' she protested, reaching the bottom of the flight and finding it impossible to resist Thane's guiding arm which led her into the sitting-room.

'If you choose to behave like a courting couple beneath a well-lit archway, then you must know that you risk being observed,' he told her cuttingly, his mouth a hard line of scorn. 'Just thank your lucky stars you weren't so irresponsible as to invite him in to spend the night with you.'

'There was never any possibility of that,' she retorted icily. 'But, since you're still so concerned about my morals, it may please you to know that I won't be going out with him again.'

'Good,' he rejoined coolly. 'Although why you expect me to believe that, when you persistently accuse me of infidelity without cause, and despite my repeated denial, I don't know! I just hope you are telling me the truth, Sapphy, because there's something else I want to know. What do you propose to do about Stephanos?'

'What do you mean?' Puzzled, she met his impatient scrutiny.

'When he awakens tomorrow and cries for you.'

'He'll be all right tomorrow! You said he wasn't badly hurt!'

'Not physically, no. Emotionally, he's torn in pieces! For God's sake, *yineka*, how can you be so blind? For the last nine months, although you've been living at Lorna's, you've visited the children every day, until now. Your absence isn't an easy thing for them to accept, however well you've tried to explain it to them. *Theos mou!*' he snapped, as she made no immediate response. 'The least you can do is to stay here tonight, and be here for him in the morning when he calls out for you.'

'I can't!' The words were forced from her lips. To prolong this agony would be too cruel for both her and the children.

'Why, Sapphira, why?' he demanded aggressively. 'Is there a reason, or is it that you still get pleasure from opposing me just for the fun of it?'

'That's not fair!' she defended herself instantly. 'I might as well ask you if you still get fun from bullying me!'

'Bullying?' His eyebrows lifted in feigned astonishment. 'When did I ever bully you, Sapphira?'

'All the time!' She faced him defiantly. 'From the moment we set foot in this house, you ordered me about as if—as if...'

'As if I loved you, and wanted you to settle down within this new and strange environment with as few problems as possible?' he interposed softly, staring at her defiant face with half-shuttered eyes.

'No!' She struggled to explain her feelings as they'd been then. 'As if I were some recalcitrant child that needed disciplining!'

'Really?' He affected a puzzled look. 'I must admit, I can't recall any such bullying.'

'You don't remember that time when we'd spent the morning picking wild flowers, and when I knocked them over accidentally you insisted I went down on my hands and knees and picked each one up separately and put it back in the basket?'

'The May Day the year after we were married?' He frowned as if trying to recall the occasion as she nodded.

'We gathered a large basketful. I remember it was a glorious day, and I wanted you to take me down to the coast after lunch...'

'And I told you I couldn't spare the time because I had to work on an important program.' There was remembrance and laughter in the soft gaze that swept her face, and Sapphira knew that his original pose of forgetfulness had been just that—a pose. A tiny shiver traversed her spine, warning her, too late, that she had been incautious in quoting that particular example. If he remembered it as totally as she did...

At the time, she'd been petulant and angry because she'd wanted to enjoy the day to its full. Desperately in love, she hadn't wanted to share Thane with anything or anyone—least of all a soulless computer. In retrospect she could see that she had been spoiled and selfish. Then she had felt cheated of his attention, and had shown her disapproval by flouncing across the room, her full skirt catching the basket of wild chrysanthemums and strewing them all over the polished wooden floor.

She had already reached the door when he'd called her back, requesting that she gather them up and place them in water.

'What for?' she'd demanded angrily. 'They're only weeds. Let Ephimi pick them up and throw them away. After all, it's what we pay her for!'

She could remember Thane's cold retort as if it were yesterday. 'We pay her for being a housekeeper, not for clearing up after juvenile tantrums, Sapphy. Now, pick them up.'

She had stared at him, her heart beating nineteen to the dozen, prey to a confusing mix of emotions. One part had wanted to dare his temper and slam out of the door. What could he do? The other part had warned her that there were limits to which she could go on defying him and still maintain the happiness they enjoyed. Yet total surrender to his imperious will had been impossible for her proud spirit!

In the end she had compromised. Casting him a smile of innocent sweetness, she'd dropped to her knees, picking up the flowers with loving care. He might have brought her to her knees, but in the end she would bring him to his and emerge the final winner! She'd taken her time, humming softly to herself, aware of his eyes burning on her bent head, his fingers, which should have been intent on work, splayed on his parted thighs as she had moved closer to him, her long blonde hair touching the floor as she'd stopped, her breasts, firm and plump, burgeoning against the low neckline of her cotton dress.

'You did as I asked. You picked them all up.' He had been thinking in tandem with her, the past as clear in his mind now as it was in hers. She had only to observe the glint in his remarkable eyes, and the half-smile that turned the corners of his mouth, to know that he was picturing the scene on that sultry spring afternoon. Somehow she had to break the spell, return both of them to the harsh reality of their present situation.

'It was a long time ago...' she began, having to stop because her throat was so dry she could hardly speak.

'Four years.' He acknowledged her comment. 'You were already carrying my children, but we didn't know...' His voice softened, thickening with emotion. 'And you knelt down in front of me and raised your lovely eyes...'

'Thane—please!' She didn't want him to continue, to describe what had happened next, because it was all in the past, a magical dream which had cracked in the light of harsh reality.

'And you told me you were sorry, that you didn't want to interfere with my work...' he watched the faint flush of colour deepen in her cheeks '...and then you ran your hand up the inside of my thigh and laid your beautiful head in my lap...'

Confusion widening her eyes, her hands shaking, she drew the edges of her light jacket together. Her body was responding to his words as once it had responded to his body: warming, aching, glowing with a flow of love which she thought had dried for ever.

'There's no point in all this...' she cried out desperately.

'Oh, yes, there is.' His gaze sharpened, taunting her. 'I want to be sure you remember how it all ended.'

As if she could ever forget.

She'd won, as she'd always known she would, because Thane had been quite unable to resist her in those heady, early days. Accepting her unspoken invitation, he had pushed her to the floor, following her down and pinning her against its olive hardness with the weight of his marvellously virile body. The flowers had tumbled once more across the floor, falling across her face and over her naked skin where Thane had wrenched open the buttons of her dress.

She had cried out in protest as the hard floor had tortured her spine, and he had laughed, the triumphant, joyous outcry of a man glorying in the pleasure of his own virility and the certainty of its imminent satisfaction, swinging her up into his arms and striding across towards the door, eager to attain the privacy of their bedroom. On the threshold she had emphasised the scale of her victory, murmuring against the sweet flesh of his face, 'But what about the flowers?'

Her triumph had been complete when he'd declared forcefully—'Let Ephimi pick them up—it's what we pay her for!'

There had been no more computer work done that day. Later, much later, she'd discovered one small chrysanthemum crushed against the underside of her breast, scented with her own perfume, nourished by Thane's caresses, and had placed it carefully inside the pages of her Bible, in the Book of Acts where the story of Sapphira had first been told.

'I remember,' she said now, carefully keeping her voice devoid of expression, refraining from moistening her lips with her tongue by an almighty effort of will as Thane's eyes lingered on their dry curves. 'I also remember what happened to the flowers. Ephimi put them in water and later that evening I bound them into a wreath for the front door, so that our house and our lives would be blessed for the coming year.' Despite her resolution, her voice cracked badly. 'It should have dried out and lasted...but only a few weeks later it had all disintegrated and blown away.'

It had been a forecast of the future, only then she'd been too blind to see it.

'Sit down, Sapphy.' Thane said quietly, indicating a chair. 'There's a solution to this situation which we should consider.'

She obeyed him, more because her legs seemed to be losing the power to support her than because she was cowed by the authoritative direction, following him with troubled eyes as he moved restlessly about the room before coming to stand in front of her.

'I'll put your new apartment back on the market and you can return here to Andromeda for the next few months.'

'That's ridiculous!' Uncomprehendingly, she searched his set face, trying to detect the logic behind his extraordinary statement. 'It would make a farce of everything...'

'Haven't you already done that?' he asked bitterly.

She flinched from his accusation, acknowledging the truth behind it.

'But——' she began automatically, knowing only that every time she set eyes on him it would make it more difficult for her emotional wounds to heal.

'Hear me out first!' he snapped, glowering down at her from his considerable height, arms folded belligerently across his broad chest, his body poised arrogantly forward, every muscle primed for attack, yet held in total control. 'My plan is that we should separate the villa in much the same way as we did to the house on Konstantinos. You can have the master bedroom, and I'll sleep on the couch in the study. In the daytime, while I'm at work, you will have full run of the place. In the evenings you can retire to your room. I'm sure you'll agree that it's large enough to be adapted into a pleasant sitting-room.'

CHAPTER SEVEN

'I DON'T see the point.' Amazed by his suggestion, Sapphira couldn't hide her hostility. 'The whole idea of a legal separation was because——'

'Because you didn't want to share your life or your bed with me!' Thane interposed harshly. 'Well, owing to the legal action, there's no question of the latter, and I'm only suggesting you do the former until Victoria and Stephanos are old enough to realise that what has happened between us is nothing to do with them—that they're not responsible for the lack of love between us, and that, despite that lack, we both care deeply for them.' There were lines of strain round his stern mouth as he regarded her unhappy face. 'It seems that your efforts on Konstantinos to get them used to the idea of us living apart weren't as successful as you must have hoped. At the moment, they're totally confused—and unhappy— and I don't seem to be doing a very good job in explaining the situation to them.'

Despite the ache in her heart, Sapphira found it difficult to suppress a smile at his admission of defeat. He had always been so competent in handling problems, and she could sense his frustration at not being able to communicate with his own offspring.

'I don't know...' Twisting her hands together, she tried to calm their trembling. What Thane had said made sense. It might be unorthodox, but it would only be temporary, and it wasn't unknown for an estranged couple to share a house but indulge in no form of communication. Could she do that?

'Well?' he prompted her softly, his eyes narrowed as he watched her expressive face. 'What is more important to you—the happiness of your babies, or your own fulfilment?'

How could he be so cruel after the sacrifice she'd already made? Unless he was still labouring under the impression that she intended to elope with Michael. The fact that he'd seen them together tonight, been a witness to the passionate kiss Michael had forced upon her, wouldn't have helped towards her credibility, however strongly she had denied any interest in Lorna's brother.

'It's the same thing,' she told him proudly, her chin raised aggressively to counter his contempt. 'How long were you intending this arrangement to last?'

'How the hell should I know?' His own turbulent emotions were mirrored on his arrogant face, the edge to his voice sharply honed. 'As long as necessary—as long as we can both stand it!'

'I need time to think about it...' From the numbed recesses of her mind came the image of those innocent, sleeping baby faces. She'd persuaded herself that she could bear to let them both go. Perhaps, if she'd had no alternative, she would have found the iron will to do it, but being offered a choice, however personally traumatic, she found her resolve weakening by the second.

Thane shrugged powerful shoulders, his eyes mercilessly intent on her seated figure. 'Take as long as you like. Start tonight, and take it day by day, if that's going to make it any easier for you.'

'And my apartment—if I agree?'

'It wasn't really suitable. I hadn't realised how small it was until tonight, when I was there waiting for you. That's another good reason for you to stay. It'll give me time to put the sale of this place in hand and look around for suitable premises for both of us.' He turned away, asking abruptly. 'Would you like a drink? I'm going to have one.'

'Thank you—yes.' She accepted his offer. It would be difficult, but, with care, she could avoid seeing him, evade the powerful masculine aura of his presence, shun the dominant spirit which lurked inside his beautiful body, shut her eyes and her mind to the comings and goings of the women who would take her place—had probably already taken her place, she amended sadly. The rewards would far outweigh the slicing pain of rejection. And it wouldn't be forever.

She tried to envisage a time when the twins would be mature enough for her to play a smaller part in their lives without too much trauma, but found it impossible. She would have to play it by ear. Already heavy with guilt at the way she had disrupted their lives, she knew that, this time, she must be prepared to guarantee them the stability they needed—and for as long as it was necessary and practicable.

Momentarily Thane's hand touched her own, as he offered her a glass with a generous measure of brandy swirling in its bowl.

'Do we have a bargain, Sapphy? Will you be here tomorrow morning, when Stephanos wakes and cries for you?'

He was asking her two questions in one, and she was bright enough to recognise how deliberately loaded he had made the second half, but, in any case, there was only one answer necessary.

'Yes,' she said quietly. 'Provided you honour the spirit of the separation order, it's a bargain.'

He didn't speak, but she couldn't miss the bright flare of satisfaction which gleamed in his brilliant eyes, or the way his shoulders squared in victory, before he leant towards her and chimed his glass against her own.

Ten minutes later, the brandy still a burning memory on her tongue, she undressed slowly, finding one of her nightdresses still in the drawer where she had left it when she'd first vacated the room. As if drawn by forces over which she had no control, she slipped the flimsy mauve georgette over her naked shoulders, moving as if in a trance to the full-length mirror which covered one door of the fitted wardrobe, and stared, unblinking, at her image.

The stay in Konstantinos had done her good. She touched one bare shoulder, trailing her fingers across the adjacent collarbone, surprised and gratified to discover that the outstanding ridge had become smoothed by flesh. Her breasts, too, appeared to have regained their shape and fullness, and her eyes no longer seemed as dull as she remembered, while the heavy downward lines that had bisected the distance between nose and chin had almost disappeared entirely!

Of course, her hair was still dreadful—straw where once it had been silk—but there was no doubt that her physical appearance was improving. She shuddered, recalling Thane's distaste at the sight of her body on the last occasion he had taken her to his bed. A sharp cry burst from her lips as a brisk knock sounded on the outside door.

Grabbing her discarded jacket and hastily pulling it over her bare shoulders, she opened the door a fraction, knowing her caller had to be Thane and resenting his intrusion into her privacy.

Wasn't it bad enough that he had persuaded her to stay, without his reinforcing his victory by disturbing her when all she wanted was to fall into bed and get some sleep?

'You never did come to collect your birthday cards, Sapphy.' He held out several envelopes of assorted sizes to her. 'It's a little late, but then, good wishes have no expiry date, do they?'

She thanked him stiffly, glad when he made no excuse to stay, and returned to sit on the double bed, tired to the point of exhaustion but intrigued enough to sort through her post. One from her parents, the next from David and Marcia, and another one from Lisa, her best friend at college. That left a further three. She recognised the handwriting of her godmother and her paternal aunt, both of whom had sent humorous cards with short chatty letters enclosed. None of them knew the state of her marriage, although her parents knew she had been unwell and spent a short time in a clinic.

As far as they were concerned, that was nearly two years previously, and she was now fully recovered and back in the bosom of a happy family. It was an illusion she had gone to great trouble to maintain, although, of course, now she would have to tell them the truth. Among them, Abby alone would be neither shocked nor surprised. Which brought her to the last card.

Her sister's writing was unmistakable. Neat and legible, as befitted a teacher. A similar envelope had arrived on her previous birthday, and, prior to that, in the previous August there had been "the letter". There had also been two Christmas cards that slotted neatly into the time between the present day and the moment when Abby had betrayed her trust and affection by encouraging Thane in his betrayal.

She didn't want to remember, but the chain of thought proved too strong to abort as she stared, unseeing, at her sister's beautiful script. Things had been going wrong for a long time between Thane and herself, she admitted painfully—ever since she'd returned to the hospital with the twins. In retrospect, she could see more clearly that she had to take her share of the blame for that. Unintentionally, she must have been hell to live with! And Abby's unexpected arrival had confused and upset her as she had struggled to be the hostess she had known that Thane expected, and had failed miserably in her attempts.

She'd been at breaking point even before the dreadful day when she'd walked into the splendid sitting-room and discovered Abby in a close embrace with Thane, her hands clutching his shoulders as if he were a long-lost lover. And he, himself, had been no reluctant recipient of her sister's passion—she had seen that for herself!

To her consequent shame, she'd launched herself on to the startled couple, screaming like a prisoner under torture, striking out at her sister with frenzied hands, while her tongue had twisted round words of accusation in terms she'd never thought to speak aloud.

And above her screams, she had heard Thane's voice, harsh and agonised, saying over and over again, 'It's not Abby's fault! I asked her to come.'

They had called a doctor and she'd been taken to the clinic. At first she had thought she'd been committed to an asylum to spend the rest of her days in imprisonment, and she'd lain there, staring at the ceiling, refusing to eat or drink, just waiting to die. Gradually, though, she'd responded to treatment, accepting that she'd been physically ill, and that, now the disruption to her hormones had been diagnosed, she could be permanently cured.

Still she'd refused to see either Thane or Abby, remembering how well they had got on together the first time they'd met, and again later when she and Thane had spent the first Christmas after their hurried wedding back in England. Pretty, lovable Abby, closer in age to Thane with a disposition and charm that ensured her popularity among both sexes. Abby, whom she'd loved and trusted...

Only her daily contact with the twins, whom Thane had continued to bring to the clinic, and Lorna's cheerful presence had comforted her in those dark hours, and by the time she had been discharged Abby had long since returned to England.

Always Thane had denied loving Abby as anything other than a sister-in-law, telling her, if she wouldn't accept his word, to read the letter Abby had left for her, which would confirm what he was telling her, but she'd refused to believe him. Full of hurt pride, she'd flung it, unopened, to the back of her dressing-table drawer. It was then that she had demanded a divorce and been met with Thane's cold refusal even to consider the idea.

So the months had gone by, in an atmosphere of bitterness and distrust, with no physical contact between them until the historic day she'd gone too far, lifting her hand at some invoked taunt and slashing it across Thane's hard cheek. Up until then he'd been restrained, cold and courteous, distant. But her action had broken the last remaining thread of his tether.

'Endaxi!' he'd grated between gritted teeth. 'If that's the way you want it, my love...'

Terrified of the dark power she'd evoked, convinced that he was about to murder her, she had fought him with every ounce of her strength as he'd half dragged, half carried her into the master bedroom, throwing her on the bed and tearing the clothes from her body.

'Thane! No, for God's sake, not like this!' Her screams muffled by the weight of his body, she'd squirmed beneath him, rolling and panting in a frenzy of movement. It had been many, many months since she'd shared his bed or been his lover, and the prospect of a coupling forced on her as a punishment filled her with a deep fear.

'What other way is there,' he'd asked, his eyes glazed behind the sweep of dark lashes, his voice husky and broken, 'when you call me a liar and a libertine and refuse to listen to reason? If I wait for you to come to me, I shall wait for ever!'

He'd already been aroused and her movements had increased his excitement.

'That's right, my angel,' he'd said, curiously tender as his hands had trembled against her flesh. 'Fight me if you must, but when the time is right you'll surrender to me, let me make you my prisoner...'

Despite her apprehension, her body had quickened to the long-remembered magic of his touch, softened and expanded to receive him, and she had welcomed him in the role of conqueror, reluctant willingness glowing in the depths of her eyes, on the twist of her lips, on the upward thrust of her breasts and in the voluptuous movements of her hips.

'Oh, dear God!' Months later, she could still recall the unearthly excitement which had claimed her that night; her certainty that, somehow, this near-violent act of passion was about to expunge every atom of the past; that afterwards, satiated and content, they would be able once more to face the future together; that no woman would ever be able to take Thane away from her again once their bodies were re-joined in the celebration of love...

'Sapphy...' Her name had been a heavy caress on his lips as he'd feasted his eyes on her, dragging his gaze in slow appreciation over her, devouring her with a terrible hunger that had promised her ecstasy in its appeasement, and then—he'd paused, his glance riveted to the mark of the surgeon's knife: the scar, which lay like the mark of a scimitar blade on the gently rounded slope of her lower abdomen.

If she lived to be a hundred, she would never forget the look of utter disgust which had replaced the dreamy gaze of desire, or the evidence of his body which confirmed his total rejection of her. Sensitive to his every reaction, she'd whimpered in distress, crawling away, her body aching, her heart so shattered that the tears which might have eased it were stillborn.

Late though it was, she'd struggled into T-shirt and jeans and fled to Lorna to seek sanctuary. The following morning, Thane had left a message for her. Although he would still not countenance a divorce, he would agree to a legal separation.

That entire process had taken nine months—a gestation period so ironical that it would have been funny if the outcome had been less tragic; and here she was, back in the marital bed—alone, tired to the point of exhaustion, with the probability of achieving sleep against her.

She fingered Abby's card thoughtfully. Strange that her sister still persevered. She found the card in her hands before she had even realised she'd ripped the envelope open. A beautifully designed bouquet of flowers, the formal wish for a happy birthday and successful year and the simple signature—"Your loving sister Abigail."

Had she really misjudged the situation all those months ago? It wasn't the first time such a thought had occurred to her, but she'd consistently suppressed it, afraid of fooling herself into believing what she so desperately desired to believe.

Taking a deep breath to steady herself, she made a decision. Aware that her pulse had quickened at the prospect, she took the letter from the drawer, returning to the comfort of the bed, propping up the pillows behind her, forcing herself to be calm. After so much suffering, surely, she must be growing impervious to pain? But her heart was thumping disquietingly against her ribs as she slid her finger beneath the flap of the envelope and eased it open. In her neat hand, Abby had written:

I have asked Thane to give you this when you are feeling better. Darling Sapphy—thank God he asked me to come to Greece when he did. He phoned me, you know, and told me he was worried sick about you, that he thought you might be having some kind of breakdown, but that the local doctor seemed unconcerned. He begged me to come and see you, talk to you, because we used to be so close and you might confide in me.

Oh, Sapphy! I was so shocked when I saw you. Even with the rotten time you'd been through I knew you shouldn't have been as depressed as that, so I phoned Marcia and told her your symptoms and she agreed with what I suspected—that you were suffering from a rare form of post-natal depression which had been allowed to go on for far too long, and needed immediate and specialised treatment.

Thane was devastated when I told him, blaming himself for not acting sooner, but how could he have? The whole thing was right outside his experience. He wept, Sapphy. He won't thank me for telling you, but that's what happened. He sat down in that chair and cursed himself for what he'd done to you and then he wept—the hard, strangled sobs of a man who's never known the comfort of tears. And I cried too, Sapphy, because of both your pains! And then I held out my arms to him, and soothed him as if he were one of my pupils, and he held on to me like a little boy whose world has fallen apart ... and that's when you came in ...

By the time you read this you'll be well. The specialist treating you is using the most modern methods and is confident that you will soon be returned to your normal vibrant health! Darling Sapphy, I *do* understand why you don't want to see me at the moment, and, since I can do nothing here, I'm going back to England today, confident that you will soon realise that the only love that your husband and I share—is for you!

Thane had wept for her? Puzzled, Sapphira brushed her warm forehead with the back of her hand. She'd been convinced that he had hated her—what she'd become. The sharply appraising glances had been criticism, surely? The lowering frowns, the terse replies and the searching questions, had all been a form of cross-examination to test her capabilities of being a wife and mother, hadn't they? She'd failed him miserably. Seduced him, trapped him, and then been unable to bear his children with ease, or nurture them with skill. He'd had every right to detest her!

She had accepted that she'd been ill—but a lot of women suffered from the baby blues, didn't they, and recovered without treatment? Hadn't her collapse shown that she was too immature, too unsuitable, to remain married to a man like Thane? She'd returned from the clinic, cured of her medical depression, but convinced that he no longer loved her. She had spurned his protestations of loyalty, and refused to share his bed because she knew, and was ashamed, of her own ugliness.

Oh, dear God! Whom had she wanted to punish? Thane, or herself, for failing him so bitterly as a wife?

If only she could have those early days back again, she would never make the same mistakes again. Instinctively, she knew that her sister had written nothing but the truth. Closing her eyes, letting the letter fall from her hands, she turned out the light. Wise, generous Abby had written that Thane loved her. But that had been close to two years ago. Since then, they'd exchanged a myriad insults, and taken part in a legal battle from which each had emerged a loser: the shoddy fabric of their relationship exposed to a group of strangers, the tattered threads of their once glorious loving displayed for judgement.

Now they shared an uneasy peace—but love? That was lost forever. She'd left her growing-up too late, and the only trump card she'd ever held in the game of love— the perfection of her body—had been taken from her as the result of giving birth to Thane's children. If he'd loved her, he wouldn't have noticed her disfigurement that dreadful evening, but the eyes of lust had been more discriminating.

With a barely muffled cry of distress she buried her face in the soft pillow, breathing in the sweetly scented linen, realising, with a feeling of hopelessness, that Thane must have been so sure of her agreement to stay that he'd arranged for the bedroom to be made ready for her. From the feel and scent of it, even the nightdress she wore had recently been laundered.

Unable to get comfortable, she drew her knees up towards her chest, assuming the foetal position. In the early carefree days of their marriage, Thane and she had often slept "spooned" together like that, his hand on her breast, the weight and power of his body a warm, insistent presence locked round her, possessive and protective... If only she had accepted his assurances when she'd returned from the clinic, been adult, confident and loving enough to believe him, she could have salvaged her marriage! Instead, she had encouraged its decay.

These thoughts were getting her nowhere! On an impulse, she sat up, reaching for her handbag in the light from the half-shuttered window. Probing fingers found that which she sought. With a little sigh of pleasure, she took the porcelain egg from the case in which it had lain since she'd received it. It fitted neatly into her palm. Sinking back once more against the pillows, her thumb tracing the outline of the little Cupid, following the curve of his wing, the arch of his bow, the deadly straight line of his arrow, she waited with patient resignation for sleep to release her, if only temporarily, from her anguish.

Hours later, awakened by a brisk knocking at her door, Sapphira struggled to sit up, brushing the hair away from her face, seeing from the shafts of sunlight which illuminated the room that the day was well under way. In response to her invitation to come in, Thane entered, his son riding astride one dark-clad hip.

'The culprit wants *your* forgiveness, too!' he announced, the dark glint of humour in his eyes offsetting the brusqueness of his voice. 'We're just on our way down to breakfast. I've asked Ephimi to bring you up a tray.'

'Thank you,' she returned stiffly, her arm going round the child as Thane dumped him unceremoniously on the bed, her eyes eagerly searching his small face for signs of injury, and finding nothing to alarm her. 'We'll have to work out a proper routine for the future if we go ahead with what we spoke about last night.'

'That shouldn't be difficult. I'm out a lot. We should be able to avoid each other without a great deal of difficulty.'

'Yes.' She made the reply stiltedly, wanting to drag her eyes away from the tall man looking down at her with total indifference, and finding it impossible. Shirt only half-buttoned, sleeves rolled up to the elbows displaying tanned, sinewy forearms, he must have been in the process of dressing when Stephanos had awakened. He'd shaved, but his dark hair was tumbled as if he'd been running his fingers through it. The ache in Sapphira's chest was so strong that she placed her hand against it. How bitterly ironical that feelings which had been dormant for so long should choose this time to stir into life. She'd supposed them completely dead, incapable of resurrection, but they seemed determined to prove her wrong.

'What's this, Mummy?'

The small body in her arms had wriggled free. Comforted by her close embrace, Stephanos had quickly returned to normal spirits, and he'd burrowed beneath the light sheet which covered her. Emerging, he opened his palm to display the porcelain egg.

Flustered, Sapphira took it from him. 'It's a present, darling. It must have fallen out of my handbag.'

'Can you eat it?' the child persevered curiously.

'No!' Sapphira laughed, taking it from his hand and placing it on the bedside table. 'It's just something beautiful to look at and enjoy.' Conscious of Thane's brooding silence, she added a little desperately, 'Your father gave it to me.'

Immediately, Stephanos's face brightened. 'Then he's forgiven you, too!' he exclaimed. 'He wouldn't have given you a present if he'd still been cross with you for going away and leaving us!'

'It's not quite like that, darling...' Looking at his eager little face, she wished she could remember what it was like being three and a half. How much of what had happened would he understand? How much should she try to tell him? 'Daddy and I think it would be nice if some time soon we had two homes, instead of just one,' she said, a trifle desperately. 'I—I went away to see if it was a good idea.'

'And it wasn't!' he crowed happily. 'Now you're back, you can come and push Vicki and me on the swing!'

'If you sit on it properly as you were told.' She looked at him sternly, glad that he hadn't pursued the subject of her absence, but feeling a twinge of despair as she realised how difficult it was going to be to prepare both children for her permanent departure. It might be several years before the time was right...

'Why don't you go and find your sister?' Thane suggested calmly. 'There'll be plenty of time for swing-pushing later in the day.'

'You're not going away again?' Eyes so like Thane's that she caught her breath at their innocent beauty surveyed her anxiously, as the little boy, having obeyed his father's suggestion and scrambled down from the bed, paused by the doorway.

'Not for a long time.' Before Sapphira could answer Thane had taken it upon himself to reassure his son. 'Not while you and Vicki still want her here with you.'

A wave of guilt washed over her. 'Do you think it was wise to say that to him?' she asked tentatively, as the small figure disappeared and they could hear his voice calling his sister's name.

'I would hardly have said it if I didn't!' Thane stood, shoulders hunched, hands in his pockets, staring down at her, his face grim. 'We've got to take this thing gradually. Last night was a traumatic experience for everyone concerned. Stephanos may have appeared his normal self just now, but that was only because he was assured when he woke up that you'd heard of his accident and had come back!

'Look, Sapphy.' His voice was soft, but she sensed the irritation behind his conciliatory manner. 'This isn't easy for any of us. There's no set formula we can follow. In the meantime, since you've agreed to share this house with me on a strictly platonic basis, we have to have some ground rules.'

CHAPTER EIGHT

SAPPHIRA met his challenging eyes with a brief nod. 'Please continue; I'm sure you've already worked something out.'

His tone was smooth and persuasive. 'Indeed. The first rule being that we don't argue in front of the twins. They have to understand that whatever the future holds for them, it was the result of a joint decision between both of us.'

'That's fair enough.' She nodded.

'The second one is that we should have one day a week together as a family in a social sense.'

'You mean, eat together?'

'I mean everything—except sleep together,' he confirmed drily.

'I—I'm not sure I can go through with this.' The desperation she felt at being forced into close proximity with him was clearly apparent in her hesitant speech. 'You're changing the terms all the time!'

'Only for the sake of our children.' He regarded her stonily. 'It was you who wanted to break up the family— well, you've succeeded. If you find the resulting debris painful to walk on, that's something you have to come to terms with.'

Sapphira looked away. 'The family was broken up anyway. I only wanted to regularise the situation.'

His angry expellation of breath forced her attention back to his dark face. 'You wanted to steal my children from me!'

'No!' She winced at his anger. 'I never thought of it in those terms!' Her shoulders lifted, and fell heavily, echoing her despair.

'You believed I didn't love them?' His voice was like dark velvet, his gaze holding hers, his face taut with barely leashed emotion.

For a brief time that was exactly what she'd believed. He'd seemed indifferent to their needs, content to leave them in Spiridoula's care, sleeping in the small hours of the morning while Sapphira had sat beside the twin cots listening to each soft breath, terrified lest the rhythm changed. Now that it was too late, she was prepared to admit that her anxiety had been the result of her illness, and that she had been over-zealous.

'I thought you had other interests.' She managed to retain her composure, although her nerves were stretched to breaking point. The last thing she wanted was to start the day with a quarrel.

Thane gave a short laugh. 'Of course, my extra-marital affairs! But you flatter me if you believe I could sustain a level of involvement with those which would exclude the children's interests entirely.'

His expression was pitiless, yet still disturbingly attractive, the cynical acceptance of her repeated accusations of the past bringing an unwelcome touch of colour to her cheeks.

'That may have been true once, but I have changed my mind,' she retorted defiantly, her flush deepening at his critical regard, her eyes darkening with pain. 'If—if it gives you any pleasure to hear me admit it—I accept that you and Abby were never romantically involved.'

'Do you, indeed?' The moss-green eyes lowered, dwelling on her soft mouth, before encompassing her pale shoulders and following the dipping V-line of her nightdress. 'Oh, yes, Sapphira *mou*, it gives me intense

satisfaction to hear you admit that you were mistaken.
I'm only sorry it took you so long to accept my word
and Abby's assurances.'

'I—I had never read the letter she wrote to me,' she
confessed unhappily. 'At least, not until last night. It—
it made a difference. It helped me to see things more
clearly.'

He said something in Greek she couldn't understand,
but the expression on his face left her in no doubt as to
his exasperation. 'I married a child when I made you
my wife,' he added darkly, confirming her impression
of his aggravation.

She couldn't deny it. She thought sadly that she'd done
a lot of growing up in the last few months, particularly
since she'd faced the horror of voluntarily losing custody
of both her children.

'It's too late to change your mind now.' His voice had
a cutting edge to it as it broke into the silence she'd
maintained. 'I won't let you play about with the children's lives any more. You made your decision last night
and I expect you to stand by it.'

She looked at the hard thrust of his jaw, the harsh
line of his mouth, and met his icy gaze with a proud lift
of her head.

'I'm just not sure what you hope to achieve with your
"family day".'

'A truce on hostilities?' he suggested, and she could
hear his impatience. 'For God's sake, Sapphira, we
managed the occasional meeting on Konstantinos
without coming to blows, didn't we? All I'm asking is
that one day a week—and clearly Sunday is the best
one—we show our children that we are able to be civil
to each other. Hopefully, by the time we finally have
separate residences, they'll feel free to confide in each
of us equally without any feelings of betrayal. As for

the rest of the week—there's no need for either of us to set eyes on the other. I'm sure we can arrange a routine of putting the children to bed to avoid a clash at their bedroom door!' His eyes sharpened a little, studying her, waiting for her reaction.

She hated the sarcastic lilt to his words, an intense flash of anger making her fingers curl up inside her fists. In their short, turbulent relationship she had been the only one to strike a blow, and it wasn't anything she was proud of. Yet didn't Thane have to bear some of the blame? He had taunted and incited her, using his natural arrogance and authority to rouse her to fury.

'I'm sure we can,' she agreed, pleased with the coolness of her response. 'I'm just rather surprised that you should want to spend so much time in my company.'

'Oh, I think I can force myself to share the same room as you once a week, *agape mou*, without flinching too noticeably.' His keen, penetrating green eyes missed nothing, burning into her upturned face until she felt she was asphyxiating. His gaze didn't waver, mesmerising her with a spell she was unable to break. He was so close that she could have put out a hand and touched him, and suddenly the sight of the hard lean body she had known so intimately in such near approximation to her had the blood pounding in her veins, revitalising her nervous system, sending repercussions through every cell of her body, so that her breasts ached in an unmistakable signal of physical arousal.

She could have wept with chagrin at the cruelty of nature. For months she'd been locked in an icy state of emotional isolation and now, when she least wanted it, it was as if a thaw had set in, releasing with it the mental pain she had tried so hard to bury in the past. Even the ironical endearment by which he'd addressed her added to her misery—*agape mou*—my love!

She closed her eyes, breaking the tension between them, holding her lids so tightly that they ached. That was a discomfort she could deal with.

'But it seems that you may have to work a little harder at accepting my presence, *ne*?' She heard his soft laugh. 'Try it, Sapphira, for the sakes of Stephanos and Victoria. You always were a splendid actress. I'm sure you can cope. After all, it's only a temporary solution—you can console yourself by looking forward to your final release, can't you?'

She didn't answer the rhetorical question, turning her head away, praying that he'd simply leave her, now that he'd made his decisions known. It was only when she heard the door open and close softly again that she was able to relax, telling herself that she was delighted he hadn't dared to touch her, ruthlessly dismissing the incredible surge of disappointment she had experienced at his quiet departure.

Final release, indeed! She hugged her raised knees, leaning forward so that her long, untamed hair streamed across them. Divorce was final, but not this legal separation into which she'd allowed herself to be trapped!

Three weeks later she had to admit that for the first time in over three years a feeling of peace and contentment hung over the Villa Andromeda.

During weekdays Thane left the house early, after having breakfast with the children. Latterly she hadn't been able to resist standing at her bedroom window watching him walk down the path to his car, memories tugging at her heart, as she found herself admiring his athletic stride, the positive carriage of his proud head on broad shoulders. He deserved better than she had given him, she admitted painfully.

If he hadn't had such a sense of responsibility, he would have walked out of her life instead of marrying her. It wasn't even as if he'd made her pregnant, although that had been more luck than judgement, she remembered ruefully. But he hadn't even waited to find out, announcing his intentions as if they were part of a pre-arranged plan instead of an instant reparation for taking—no, that was wrong—*accepting* her virginity as a New Year present, and in her adolescent immaturity she had believed he loved her!

Since living in Greece, she had become aware of the nature of the self-esteem which motivated Greek men, its essence being inviolability and freedom. Known as *philotimo*, it was more honour than pride: basic to a Greek's personal being, his status within a family, village and district. Too late, she had realised it was Thane's *philotimo* which had dictated his assertion of marriage. Of course, she should have refused him. Instead she had accepted, and in so doing had ruined both their lives.

Turning from her most recent sojourn at the window, she began to dress, choosing turquoise linen trousers and a sleeveless shirt top which she knotted round her midriff.

True to his promise, Thane had turned the main bedroom into a comfortable sitting-room for her, with an additional armchair and table, bookcase and television set. It was here that she took refuge every evening just before six when Thane was usually expected home. On the occasions when he stayed out later, he always made a point of leaving word with Ephimi, so she was able to rearrange her own day around his absence.

Today was to be one of those days, she reminded herself as she applied a light make-up to her face, giving her plenty of time to take the twins for a walk to the nearby cluster of village shops in the morning, followed by a play session in the garden before lunch. Afterwards she'd pay a short visit to Lorna while the twins had their afternoon siesta.

Then, when she returned, while Spiridoula supervised the children's tea she could continue on the portfolio of fabric design she was compiling. Thane's suggestion that she might like to use some of her spare time using the graphic programs available on the ultra-sophisticated computer in his study, in pursuance of the career she'd once contemplated, had astounded her.

Although she'd often longed to use her creative talents, it had never occurred to her that Thane would countenance his wife's working, or encourage her in any pursuit that might lead to that end. Of course, things were different now, she admitted. But, still, his casual suggestion had elated her and his offer to show any portfolio she produced to his friend—Andreas Constanidou—who headed up Constanidou Textiles—had had her gasping with shock and pleasure. It had been all she could do not to throw her arms around his neck and kiss him!

As a therapy, she admitted, brushing back her hair and plaiting it before turning it into a coil at the back of her head, it couldn't have been better! Entranced by the sheer scope of the "paint" facility, with its palette of over two thousand colours and its capability of pattern repeat and over-printing, she had approached her self-appointed task with a glowing enthusiasm, leaving the study reluctantly each evening before Thane's arrival, having carefully cleared away every trace of her occupancy, her mind still abuzz with new ideas.

She could already hear the children's voices as she ran lightly down the stairs to join them at the dining table. Engrossed in their own conversation, they didn't even acknowledge her arrival as she pulled out her own chair and subsided on it. How could anyone even dream of splitting them up? If that judge or mediator or whatever the Greeks called him could have seen them like this, he would have realised the cruelty of his proposition!

Looking at Victoria's fair head so close to Stephanos's dark one, she felt her early elation of the morning dwindle away. If she thought she would ever get used to losing them, she was fooling herself!

'Mummy, can we have a little cat?' It was her daughter who was the first to recognise her presence, turning an excited face towards her.

'Parakalo, Mummy, parakalo!' Stephanos added his plea, choosing to speak the language of his father, his eyes of the same malachite brilliance as his sire's. 'Angelia's cat has had four and she can't keep them all. Daddy told us last night when he came in to say *kali nichta*. He says we can have one if you don't mind.'

'You don't mind, do you, Mummy?' Was ever a child so innocent looking as the sweet Victoria when she wanted her own way?

Sapphira suppressed a smile. Between them, her *didimee* would be able to charm the devil himself. Pretending to consider the matter deeply, she left them anxiously awaiting her verdict for several seconds.

'Not if you promise to look after it yourselves,' she said at last. 'That means seeing it has fresh food put down at a regular time and plenty of fresh water. Ephimi has quite enough to do looking after us. We don't want to give her more work.'

Pouring herself out a cup of coffee from the percolator already on the table, she drank it slowly, watching the children eating their boiled eggs and bread and butter, their fresh faces lively and intent as they discussed between mouthfuls what name the proposed new member of the family should bear.

The matter was still unsettled by the middle of the afternoon, when they retired to the nursery for their customary siesta, and Sapphira set out for Lorna's flat.

Her friend greeted her cheerfully. 'Sapphy! You look wonderful!'

'Hardly that!' Sapphy laughed at the compliment. 'But I must admit your advice was worth taking. I look less like an old hag than I did a couple of months ago!'

'You never looked an old hag, my dear.' Lorna surveyed the younger girl critically. 'Just over-tired and over-bleached by the sun. I take it, you're not regretting your decision to return to Thane?'

'Not to Thane!' Sapphy denied it vigorously. 'I've returned to the villa, that's all. It's not the same thing at all. In fact, we barely see each other.'

'Which is a great deal different from seeing each other barely, eh?' Amused, Lorna watched the flush which mounted Sapphira's cheeks. 'My dear girl, how charming it is to see you blush. Are you trying to tell me that there's no prospect of a reconciliation on the cards?'

'Reconciliation?' Sapphira swallowed hard. 'No, of course not. How could there be? We're legally separated!'

'And living under the same roof. You mean to tell me you don't spend any time together?'

From anyone else Sapphira would have resented the questions, but Lorna was her confidante and friend, and she knew, despite Thane's brooding dislike of her, that the older woman truly had her, Sapphira's, interests at heart. Without her support during those dreadful days in hospital, and afterwards when Thane had so cruelly rejected her and she'd fled for sanctuary, she couldn't imagine where she might be now. She shrugged her shoulders.

'We spend each Sunday together as a family day. It was Thane's idea. He thought it would be good for the children to see us together as friends.'

'Mm.' Lorna pursed her lips uncommittedly. 'And are you? Friends, I mean?'

'In a way I suppose we are, yes.' Sapphira sank down in one of Lorna's soft armchairs. 'We don't argue in front of the twins, and both of us go out of our way to be polite to the other and avoid contentious subjects.'

'It sounds enthralling,' Lorna responded drily. 'I'm sure the twins are very happy with the situation, but what about you—and Thane?'

'I imagine he's bored, but he puts a good face on it.'

'And you—what about you, Sapphy—is it what you want?'

'I want...' Sapphira began, then stopped, blindingly aware of her desire. She wanted to put the clock back to the time when she and Thane had been lovers, immersed in each other to the exclusion of everything else. That time of false illusion when she'd been ecstatically happy. She wanted a chance to make reparation to him, to earn the love she'd never won. '...I don't know.' Unable to tell Lorna the truth, she lied.

Lorna's face changed, amusement dying from her eyes, leaving them sad and knowing. 'You're still in love with him, aren't you, Sapphy?'

'No!' She rejected the idea too quickly. 'He doesn't want me.' She stared down at her hands, humiliated by her confession.

'There's no connection between those two statements, you know.' Lorna stared at her bent head. 'It's true what Michael told me, isn't it? He doesn't stand a chance with you?'

'I like him as a friend...' Sapphira made a helpless gesture with both hands. 'He's sweet and kind, and the last thing I want to do is hurt him, but...'

'He's not the man for you.' Lorna finished the sentence for her. 'Yes, I was certain he didn't stand a chance. I'm sure the decision he's made is the right one.'

'Decision?' Puzzled, Sapphira waited for an explanation, curling up on Lorna's comfortable sofa as she did so.

'Yes; he didn't want to embarrass you by phoning or calling at the villa, so he asked me to tell you the good news. He's accepted a marvellous opportunity to move the restaurant from Kethina to Athens itself. It's what he's always wanted since its reputation outgrew its capacity. Up until now, he just hasn't been able to release enough capital to make the move and expand as well, but he's had an offer from an Athens hotelier who is prepared to put up the money involved and remain a sleeping partner. Michael and his partner have gone very thoroughly into it and they're convinced that, even with a third partner, the profit potential is enormous!'

'But that's fantastic!' Sapphira's face shone with joy. 'Oh, I know how much that's going to mean to him. How did he meet this man?'

Lorna shrugged. 'Apparently he'd heard of the restaurant's reputation and, having visited it on several occasions, he decided it had the makings of a goldmine if it could be more centrally located. The thing is, my dear,' she continued quietly, 'Michael wants me to go to Athens with him and work from there.'

'Well, of course, you must!'

'That's what I'd decided.' Lorna nodded. 'But I'm delighted to hear you say it. I wouldn't want you to think I was deserting you, but if you ever need me, well, Athens is only a little further along the road, and you'll always be welcome.' She smiled wryly. 'Now that you and Thane have signed a peace treaty, you won't need a sanctuary on your doorstep, will you?'

'No.' Sapphira returned her clear-eyed gaze. 'I won't, but I'll always want to be your friend and visit you and bring the children. I'll never forget what I owe you, and Michael too. I wish you both all the joy and happiness and luck you deserve!'

Lorna smiled. 'If Michael had believed that he had had any future with you, I don't think he would have agreed, but as it is I'm sure we've all made the right decision. Let's have a cup of tea, shall we? Then I can bring you up to date on all the arrangements.'

It was early evening when Sapphira re-entered the Villa Andromeda and made her way to Thane's study. Within minutes she was deeply engrossed in what had become a consuming interest. Because the computer was able to miniaturise designs and apply them as paint to designated surfaces, she'd even copied simple shapes of both clothes and furniture as applicable, covering them with the designs she had created. Printed out on Thane's first-class printer, the results were excellent. Soon, she thought delightedly, she'd have a large enough portfolio to present to Thane—and, if he approved of her work, there was the exciting prospect of the introduction to his friend.

'That's very impressive!'

Swivelling at the sound of the deep voice behind her, Sapphira caught her breath in a gasp. Deeply concentrating, she hadn't heard the door open, and the first intimation she had of Thane's presence was when she heard his voice at her shoulder.

'Oh!' A small panicky sensation rose inside her, as if she'd been caught doing something nefarious. 'I'd no idea how late it was!' She stopped the printer in midstream, only to find her hand grasped and drawn away from the keyboard as Thane reactivated the print program.

'I'm not in the mood to prosecute trespassers tonight,' he said equably, his hand still firmly capturing her own. To her consternation, he reached with his free hand for the nearly complete portfolio, beginning to turn the pages with careful deliberation.

Her hand stiffened in his hold as she tried to release herself. His silence was ominous, filling her with doubts, as every nerve in her body came on edge. He mustn't see the effect he had on her! Her legs trembling...a tightness in her chest. Suppose he decried her work as useless?

'They're just preliminary ideas,' she blurted out, her eyes fixed on his classic profile. 'Of course, I've been away from the business for a long time...'

'Hmm.' His eyes returned to her anxious face. 'I'm not qualified to give a professional opinion—but my personal opinion is that you've mastered the medium with great dexterity, and your work shows flair and imagination.' He released her hand as the printer stopped. 'Now you can switch it off.'

'Thank you.' She was grateful, both for his permission to stop her labours and his unqualified praise of her work, a warm glow of pleasure softening the contours of her face as she hastily gathered up her bits and pieces.

'Sapphy—before you go...I need your co-operation in a business matter.'

'Yes?' Her arms full of the portfolio and assorted pens and papers, she paused on her way to the door. His tone had been peremptory, offering her no choice. A premonition of unease swept away her previous euphoria as she waited for him to continue.

Stepping closer to her, he regarded her with an urbane, yet guarded, speculation, before a slight cryptic smile touched his mouth. 'I have an important dinner engagement tomorrow evening and I want you to be there with me.'

For a split second she was stunned at his audacity, then pride came to her aid.

'No, I won't do it, Thane,' she told him coldly. 'I'm living here under sufferance, for the children's sake, and our agreement only calls on me to share your company on Sundays.' She saw his mouth tighten ominously as a flicker of anger darkened his eyes, and carried on recklessly. 'What's wrong with asking Angelia, as you usually do? Or has she got another date?'

'On this occasion Angelia isn't suitable.' He rammed his hands into his pockets and glared down at her, his legs braced apart, his whole attitude belligerent. 'My contact is an Englishman, name of Robinson. His wife is with him, and they've particularly asked to meet my wife. It seems Mrs Robinson comes from the same part of England as you do.'

Looking defiantly into his lean angry face, Sapphira felt her heartbeat quicken. He looked so tough and sure of himself, so confident of eventual victory, but it was too much to ask of her. She shivered, anticipating the anger that would wash over her at her refusal; but if he'd had any consideration at all for her feelings he would have known his request was impossible.

'Then you'll have to tell them that you're no longer married!' She went to move away but he grabbed her shoulder so roughly that several of the papers she was carrying fell to the floor.

'Leave them!' he grated as she tried to stoop, his other arm coming to hold her so that she was transfixed, unable to do anything but meet his steely gaze with a false bravado. 'It's too late for that,' he told her harshly. 'Besides, I *am* married, whether you like it or not.'

'In name only! And only because you refused to consider the divorce I wanted.' Trembling, she tried to dislodge herself from his hands, but without success.

'Don't beg the issue, Sapphy.' His face was so close to hers that she could smell the faint trace of aftershave on his warm skin, her senses leaping as every cell in her body responded to his nearness as if pre-programmed. 'This contract means a hell of a lot to me, the company, and, eventually, to you. The more profitable we become, the better your standard of living when we part!'

'It's no good trying to bribe me!' She was conscious of the rise and fall of her breasts beneath the thin turquoise cotton, of the inner turmoil which was shaking her slender frame. It was bad enough, this half-life she was living. How could she be expected to act the normal, loving wife, knowing all the time that Thane despised her, found her repulsive, and that when the evening ended his use for her would be over too?

Temper sparked in her eyes, the only answer she could find to the desolation which was overflowing within her. 'My answer's still no. Now, will you please let me go?'

Something flashed briefly in the sage depths of his eyes, whether fury or contempt, she couldn't be certain. For a couple of seconds she held her breath, feeling his tension, wondering if he would vent his displeasure on her in some other form. It was fear of his nameless retribution which forced her into urgent speech. 'You're contravening the separation order by using violence against me!'

'Violence?' He stared at her, his face as motionless as a carved mask. '*Theos mou!* You dare to accuse me of that? Is that what you plan—to tempt me into hurting you so that you can return to the court to claim both the children after all?' His hands dropped from her arms and he turned away, but not before she'd seen disgust for her contort his features into a grimace of pain. 'Pick your papers up and get out of here before I'm tempted to show you the true nature of violence!'

Sinking to her knees, Sapphira did as she was bid, her fingers shaking, her whole body trembling, painfully aware of the simmering anger she had aroused in the man she would once have willingly given her life for. He thought she was taking some pleasure in thwarting him. There was no way she could explain to him the impossible pain that such a masquerade would inflict on her. Her gaze flickered unconsciously upwards, absorbing the rigid line of the back view presented to her, the breadth of shoulder, the powerful, tight hips, the muscular length of his legs not disguised by the expensive suiting which garbed them. Thane: lord... liege... master....

It was only as she tasted salt in her mouth, as she scrambled to her feet and made blindly for the door, that she realised she was crying.

CHAPTER NINE

SAPPHIRA breathed a sigh of disgust the following morning as she withdrew the disk she'd been using and switched the computer off. She'd intended to continue compiling her portfolio, but all her creative instincts seemed to have deserted her.

Vaguely she registered that the doorbell had rung, too immersed in the realisation of how much the previous night's quarrel with Thane had disturbed her to wonder who might be calling.

A tap at the study door preceded Ephimi's entrance. 'It's the Kyria Andronicos. She wishes to see you.' The housekeeper looked anxious, as if she expected a rough refusal of admittance. Once, that might have been the case, but not now. Suffering had matured Sapphira—and maturity lent her some dignity.

'That's all right, Ephimi. I was just taking a rest from working. I can spare her a few moments.' Automatically her hand went to her hair, smoothing it back with nervous fingers. At one time, during her illness, she hadn't cared what she had looked like. Now she did: particularly under the appraisal of the woman who shared more of Thane's life than she did! Vanity it might be, but she was glad that her early morning despair hadn't prevented her from dressing casually but smartly in a straight white skirt with a deep pink loose-fitting top which tied neatly on her hips.

'*Kalimera*.' Angelia Andronicos returned the polite greeting before switching to English in her carefully modulated but slightly guttural voice. 'Thanos told me

135

you'd agreed to take one of my kittens.' She lifted a large cardboard box, perforated with several holes, and placed it on the desk. 'It's a little male, perfectly healthy and just weaned from its mother.' Before Sapphira could speak, she'd opened the box, reaching in to produce a grey kitten marked like a tiger cub, its bright green eyes enormous in its small pointed face, its ears long and pointed.

'Oh, he's beautiful!' Sapphira reached for the small creature, enchanted by its oriental appearance, so different from the typical British tabby.

'I expect you'll have him neutered when he's old enough,' Angelia eyed her with speculation. 'I understand it's the custom in England. Here in Greece it would be considered cruel to deprive a male of his masculinity.'

Aware of the truth of that remark, Sapphira nevertheless sensed that her visitor's comment extended beyond the narrow confines of domestic pets. Was she being accused of emasculating Thane by forcing a legal separation on him? Wasn't Angelia aware that her husband no longer desired her anyway?

Determined not to be drawn, she decided to ignore the other woman's supposition. 'The children will be thrilled,' she said instead, forcing a smile on her face. 'I'll call them in, and perhaps I could offer you some refreshment?'

'Coffee, then—thank you.' Angelia sat down, a picture of the efficient and composed businesswoman in a navy linen dress with a shawl collar and slim skirt.

Their eyes shining with excitement, Victoria and Stephanos claimed their pet with exclamations of wonder and joy, carrying him off to display to Ephimi with instructions to hand him over to her so he could be settled in and get used to his surroundings.

'They're not mauling him, are they?' Sapphira asked anxiously a few moments later, when Ephimi came in with the tray of coffee.

'Of course not!' The housekeeper looked shocked. 'They're gentle children, for all their liveliness. Spiridoula's found him a box to sleep in, and at the moment they're all watching him playing with a ping-pong ball.'

'It was kind of you to think of them,' Sapphira said politely, as Ephimi left them, pouring out a cup of coffee and handing it to her guest. 'And to go out of your way to bring him over.'

'I wanted to speak to you.' Uncompromising dark eyes challenged her over the rim of the cup. 'I understand you've refused to dine with the Robinsons this evening.'

Sapphira stiffened, her muscles tightening defensively at this breach in the rules of hospitality.

'Did Thane send you?' she asked imperiously, a cutting edge apparent in the cool tone of her voice.

Angelia's eyebrows rose. 'Kyria Stavrolakes—I am not sent anywhere! I may not have any equity in the business but I do a professional job there. I am not a messenger girl!'

'Naturally, I know that.' Sapphira refused to back down. 'On a personal level, though . . .' Jealousy was a bitter taste in her mouth.

'Ah—so it's as I thought! You *do* believe there is more between your husband and myself than official business!'

'Is there?' Pride should have kept her silent, but she'd blurted the question out without thought.

'Surely that's a question you should ask your husband?'

Was that pity she saw in the other woman's eyes? 'I have,' she returned stonily. 'He denies it.'

'And you don't believe him?' Angelia regarded her without any sign of emotion on her lovely face. 'Then you do him a grave injustice, both in doubting his word and his honour. If I have stepped into your shoes on occasions, it is solely because you have refused to fill them, and it was in the company's interests that someone should.' Her face, with its creamy skin and full-lipped mouth, remained composed. 'And those occasions to which I've referred have always been social rather than intimate.'

'But...' Sapphira paused. Could she believe Angelia's assertion? The temptation to do so was almost unbearable, because she had no real proof of Thane's infidelity. Her suspicions had been bred from a sense of inferiority, as her safe world had crumbled about her, and guilt, because she was no longer able to be the kind of wife Thane had wanted and deserved.

It was almost as if Angelia had read her tortuous thoughts.

'But,' the Greek woman took her prompt, 'you need more than my word to convince you? What else do you want to know—that I have a satisfactory liaison of my own? Believe it, then, because it's true. Other than that, the faith you need must be found in your own heart. What you should be concerned about is not the fantasy of my having seduced your husband, but the future prosperity of the company. This contract Robinson can give us is the most important project we've ever been offered. It can take us up with the high-fliers! My brother and your husband have worked very hard for a long time for an opportunity like this.' Her eyes flashed with calculated arrogance. 'To attend a dinner would seem to be a very small contribution on your part, particularly since you still reside in the family home.'

'So small, it could hardly sway a decision based on cost-effectiveness and capability, surely?' With an effort, Sapphira fought down her initial umbrage at Angelia's overt criticism.

'Possibly,' Angelia didn't deny it. 'On the other hand, it's sometimes the very small things that finally tip the balance, *ne*? The point is, Mr Robinson is a potential client and has expressed a wish to meet you. To refuse him is tantamount to a snub. The way in which you wish to express your displeasure with your husband is your own concern. When it affects my brother, I take the liberty to ask you to reconsider your decision.'

'But why should he want to meet me?' Sapphira asked uneasily. 'Why should he even know of my existence?'

'Since your photograph is so prominently displayed on Thanos's desk, he could hardly escape the knowledge,' Angelia retorted drily.

'Photograph? What photograph?' It was years since she'd stood before a camera. That Thane should have some photograph of her on view shook her badly.

Angelia's gaze softened, as if she were aware of the other girl's confusion and felt a modicum of pity for her. 'You're sitting perched on a table, wearing a scarlet dress with white trimming round the neck and long angel trumpet sleeves.'

'My wedding dress!' The words were blurted out from Sapphira's dry lips. She'd been married in early February, on a bitterly cold day, by special licence at the local register office, her outfit making a brilliant statement of colour against the winter grey of the weather. For the ceremony she'd piled her long hair on top of her head, crowning it with a narrow-crowned, sweeping-brimmed hat of matching scarlet.

At the reception, surrounded by her loving family, high on the joy of being in love, she had danced in Thane's arms, delaying the delicious moment when they would consummate their love for the first time as a married couple.

'I could dance all night!' she'd declared ecstatically later that evening, when the last guest had left, teasing him with the promise of her eyes and the subtle provocation of her sinuous body, as she'd perched on the edge of the dining table. Laughingly, she had unpinned her hair, letting it fall to her shoulders in a cloak of spun gold.

'The dancing's over, *agape mou*.' His eyes had glinted with promise, and she had shivered in delight. Then he had seized her brother's discarded camera, aiming the lens at her. 'Give me a smile while I tell you what *my* plans are until morning.'

Obediently, she had smiled, and when he'd finished telling her he'd pressed the button, before discarding the camera to carry her upstairs to the bedroom which had been so lovingly prepared for them in the deliberately emptied house.

It had been a stunning shot, and she'd supposed it was in the album with all the others. Never in her wildest dreams had she supposed that Thane had taken it and displayed it where he worked. Then she had been at her best, young and winsome, the water nymph who had captured his roving masculine eye at their first encounter. What a comparison now! Older, thinner, physically and emotionally scarred by childbirth and her own stupidity!

Sapphira shuddered. 'I'm not the same woman.'

'We all change.' Angelia regarded her thoughtfully. 'That's hardly a crime. Besides, in the eyes of those who love us, the change is imperceptible.'

'Thane doesn't love me!' The words were out before she could control them, and she found herself flushing at the gross betrayal of her pain to this woman who was neither friend nor enemy, whose interest was motivated purely on financial grounds.

Angelia finished her coffee before rising to her feet. 'As to that, I couldn't say, since he has never discussed his feelings for you. It's ironic though, is it not, that many Greek men have no wish to include their wives in their business lives, and your husband, who does, is obliged to look elsewhere when he desires feminine company?'

'We're separated . . . we lead different lives!' It was as if Sapphira were exonerating herself for some dreadful crime. 'Why should I live a lie?'

Angelia shrugged elegant shoulders. 'Why? Because Thanos needs you to. There is, after all, no one else who can take your place. A few hours? An excellent meal, good company—fellow countrymen? Is it really too much to ask?'

'Wait!' Angelia had already turned towards the door, but halted in her stride at Sapphira's urgent command. 'Perhaps it's too late. Suppose he's already turned down the invitation on my behalf?'

'He hasn't.' Was there a new warmth in Angelia's dark eyes? 'He's decided not to say anything until he arrives for dinner at their hotel. He's then going to make the excuse that you phoned at the last moment to say you had a migraine and couldn't leave the house. That way, your absence will give the least offence.'

'I've nothing to wear.' It was as if her desperation was seeking for ways of preventing her from going.

'But you have a clothes allowance, *ne*? And Athens is only a taxi ride away. You would have ample time to visit a hairdresser as well as shop before meeting Thanos.'

Angelia was right. If she wanted to do it, it could be done. The problem was, would her resolve hold out during the coming hours? Could she play the part required of her without letting Thane down? Wouldn't her absence be preferable to her presence if she presented an image so different from the vibrant, laughing girl she'd once been?

'I'll think about it,' she said at last. 'I need more time to make up my mind. You won't say anything to Thane about it, will you? If I decide to go, I'll phone him at the office before he leaves.'

'I promise not to say a word.' Angelia smiled for the first time. 'As far as your husband is aware, I've simply delivered a kitten. I wouldn't want to prejudice a good working relationship with him by admitting to interfering in his personal affairs. It just seemed too good an opportunity to miss, with so much at stake. Perhaps, in time, you will forgive my presumption. It was necessary, I think, for a little frank speaking between us in any case, *ochi*?'

Not waiting for an answer to her question, she continued smoothly, 'The coffee was delicious, and I hope the kitten brings you all much pleasure.'

She extended her hand and Sapphira took it, surprised by the firmness of her clasp. 'The Robinsons are staying at the Elixir Palace and Thanos is meeting them there—the time is seven o'clock for eight.'

Standing at the front door, Sapphira watched her unexpected visitor make her way to her parked car. It must be important for the company for Angelia Andronicos to have made a personal appeal. Perhaps if Thane's approach had been different last night she would have agreed. No, that was trying to push the blame off her own shoulders. She'd felt inadequate, unable to carry off a social engagement with the aplomb of her youth. Perhaps she had underestimated herself? And as for the other woman's assurance regarding her relationship with

Thane, with an incredible spurt of happiness Sapphira realised intuitively that Angelia had been speaking the truth, in the same way that Abby hadn't lied to her either.

With a flash of painful insight she recognised that, unable to make her marriage work, she had sought desperately to put the blame of its failure on someone else, refusing to accept Thane's assurances until, in exasperation, he had ceased to give them. What a stupid, ignorant little fool she'd been! It was too late to save her marriage, but not too late to help Thane's career if Angelia had been correct in her estimation of what was at stake. It was the least, the very least, she could do for him in reparation.

Thoughtfully she made her way to her bedroom, excitement already stirring her blood, so that when she looked in her mirror her eyes sparkled with the prospect of facing a new challenge. Her appearance had certainly improved in the last few months, she decided critically. The rest on Konstantinos, the happiness of enjoying her children, the thrill of compiling her portfolio, plus partaking of Ephimi's beautifully cooked meals—all these things had played their part in transforming the skeleton she had become into something much more presentable.

True, the bones of her face were cleanly cut, her cheekbones sharp, the sockets of her eyes deep, but her neck was no longer corded, and as for her shoulders…she touched the warm flesh beneath her top, drifting her fingers across her collarbones: gone were the ugly salt cellars which had made her look like a starved waif; and as for her breasts, their return to firm plumpness had been one of the first changes she had noticed as her bras had begun to fit perfectly once more.

With the right kind of dress it was possible that she could pass muster. She raised her hand to touch her face. Thanks to Lorna's help and advice, her skin was soft again, so no problems there. Her hair? That was dreadful, probably beyond help. Fingering it, she remembered Angelia's comments about visiting a hairdresser. Well, of course, that was a possibility.

In an agony of indecision, she turned from the mirror. Could she spend a whole evening with Thane, pretending they were still lovers? Act the devoted wife, eager for her husband's success? She could try. Go to Athens, get her hair done, buy a dress. There'd be no need to make a decision until much nearer the time. She could always change her mind, couldn't she, and there'd be no harm done?

Her mind made up, she went up to the nursery to tell the twins and Spiridoula of her decision to go into the capital.

'I'm not sure how long I'll be. It's possible I'll accept a dinner invitation, so please don't be alarmed if I'm back late.'

She cuddled the twins, stroked the kitten who had been named Tigris, and ran downstairs to tell Ephimi of her intentions.

While she was waiting for the taxi to come to collect her, she remembered her engagement ring: something she had never replaced on her finger after it had been removed when her hands had swollen in pregnancy. There was a sweet nostalgia in opening her jewellery box and lifting it from its velvet bed. A central ruby surrounded by eight diamonds sliding easily over her knuckle. A little loose, perhaps? There was another ring she could wear to hold it in place.

Wrapped in tissue paper was the ring Thane had bought for her on the birth of the twins. Never worn, it had lain in the box, half-forgotten until that moment. Carefully she exposed it to the daylight, a thick flat band of gold set Victorian-style with alternating rubies and diamonds in a half-hoop. Sick with worry in case the premature babies didn't survive, and suffering from an undiagnosed illness, she'd been in no mood to appreciate either the gift or the giver.

Dear God! How could she have been so appallingly cruel to the man she'd married, the man she'd loved? To this day, he'd never mentioned the ring, yet it must have cost him a great deal of money. Not that that would have concerned him, but how it must have hurt him to have had his gesture treated so churlishly!

Little wonder that she'd killed off every scrap of feeling he may once have had for her! Sliding it over her finger, she went downstairs to open the door to the taxi driver. If she could find the courage to go to the Elixir Palace, then she could find the courage to wear the ring!

It was midday when she arrived in Athens, finding an outside café in a tree-lined square, and ordering a pizza with a coffee before making for the main shopping area. It was while she was looking for a suitable dress that she saw the hairdressing salon. Obviously fashionable, it would be expensive, but then she needed something drastic and was prepared to pay for it.

Fortunately she was able to get an immediate appointment, and watched anxiously in the mirror as the young Greek stylist considered the extent of the problem.

She was in the chair for nearly three hours, plied with magazines and cool drinks while she detached her mind from what was being done to her.

'There!' The cry was mildly triumphant. 'You may now look, *kyria*!'

'Oh!' Startled, Sapphira found herself staring at a stranger. It was a miracle. A shining bell of hair, thick and lustrous, the ends touching her cheeks at the front, the sides, beautifully cut, dipping lower so the fall at the back touched the nape of her neck.

'The front is adaptable, you see.' A flick of the comb, and glinting strands broke the classic line of her forehead.

'My husband won't recognise me!' It was astonishing, the metamorphosis he had wrought. It was almost like being born again, taking on a new personality, leaving the agony of the past behind. Her mouth seemed fuller, more sensuous, her eyes a deeper more dominating blue. She shook her head in wonderment.

'You don't like it?' The disappointment of the man who had performed the miracle was almost comical.

'Yes, yes, I do.' Hastily she reassured him, gasping as she saw how late it was. 'How much do I owe you?'

Having paid the bill, she hurried towards a street where she knew she would find several high-class boutiques. How fortunate it was that shops in Greece stayed open late into the evening.

As soon as she saw the scarlet silk there was no doubt in her mind. A flared skirt was teamed with a draped top which extended over the hip-line of the skirt, following every slender curve of her body. There were no sleeves, but the shoulder-line was extended and fashionably padded. The beauty was in the fabric, the colour and the cut. It needed nothing to ornament it. The small gold watch she always wore, and her rings, were sufficient jewellery.

It wasn't cheap, but then it wasn't exorbitantly expensive either, by Thane's standards. She felt no qualms as she enquired about sandals and an evening bag. It was only after she'd chosen high-heeled sandals and matching slim scarlet- and gold-striped pochette, that she thought about what to wear underneath.

'We have just the thing, *kyria*.' The shop assistant reached into a drawer and produced a scarlet body-shaper. 'Lycra and lace,' she announced proudly. 'It will fit you like a second skin, and see, suspenders attached, so you may wear stockings!'

'I'll take it.' She might as well be hung for a sheep as for a lamb, Sapphira decided. If she was going to carry off this masquerade then she'd play the part to the best of her ability. 'And I'll take two pairs of your finest nylon stockings too!'

It was approaching six o'clock when she emerged from the boutique. There was no going back now, not after she'd spent a small fortune. All she had to do was tell her husband she'd changed her mind—and hope he was pleased!

Finding a public phone box, she punched in his office number and waited impatiently as it rang several times. No answer. After a few more seconds she slowly replaced the receiver. This was something she hadn't anticipated. Now there was only one thing she could do: go to the Elixir Palace, get changed there, and pray that Thane would arrive to keep the appointment—and arrive alone.

Half an hour later she discovered, much to her relief, that the lobby powder-room was spacious and unoccupied, and she changed her clothes in an ample cubicle before emerging to survey herself in the full-length mirror. Not only was she reassured about the appearance of her new dress, but it felt even more special with the body-hugging lingerie beneath it. Taking her time, she replaced her make-up from scratch, paying special attention to her eyes so that her lashes curled, thick and glossy, drawing attention to their clear sparkle. Fortunately she'd brought a lipstick with her which would match the dress. She applied it with a steady hand, blotting off the excess so that no ugly rim would be left on cutlery or crockery.

It was a quarter to seven when she emerged into the foyer carrying her day clothes, carefully folded, in the smart boutique box carrier. A quick look round established that the restaurant was on the ground floor, beyond the bar which led immediately from the reception area.

If Thane was coming, it was almost certain that he would either announce his presence at reception or walk straight through to the restaurant bar. Either way, if she were to take a seat in the lobby, she could hardly miss him. Even if he were to go directly to the Robinsons' room, he would have to cross her line of vision on his way to the lifts. Appearing more calm than she was beginning to feel, Sapphira chose an armchair from which she could keep an eye on the enormous glass doors leading to the street, and tried to relax.

Supposing he didn't come: what would she do? Retreat to Andromeda with her proverbial tail between her legs? She was a fool to have embarked on such a project without ensuring that Thane still needed her. Another glance at her watch told her there were only two minutes left before seven. She'd been sitting there alone for nearly fifteen minutes, painfully aware of the curious looks which had passed her way. Supposing the hotel manager mistook her purpose in waiting and asked her to leave? Mortification brought a shiver down her spine. Thane was never late! She'd give him two more minutes and then she'd beat a quick retreat.

It was at that precise moment, when her agitation was mounting to panic point, that she saw him, experiencing such a sense of utter relief that she let out her breath in a deep sigh as she rose to her feet.

As usual, he looked superb, head and shoulders above the other patrons milling about in the foyer. Dark-suited, a large rigid-framed briefcase in one hand, he walked with a natural authority towards the reception desk, glancing neither to right nor left. Not close enough to hear what he said, Sapphira watched, her heart in her mouth, as he handed over the briefcase with a nod and pleasant smile, before turning towards her.

If his eyes had taken a cursory picture of his surroundings, there wasn't the slightest intimation that he was aware of her presence as he went to pass her.

'Thane...' Her voice sounded husky, uncertain. She hadn't expected that she would have to accost him like this.

He stopped, turning his head in the direction of her voice. Across the two metres which separated them he stared at her as if she were a stranger.

She'd ruined the whole thing! She knew it. He must have changed his mind and told the Robinsons that she wasn't coming—or, even worse, despite Angelia's assurances, chosen to take another woman in her place to make a foursome. Either way, her presence there at that time could only embarrass him.

'I'm sorry—it's not important—I just thought—I'll go!' She backed away from his expressionless face, wishing she could evaporate into thin air.

'Sapphy?' He seemed unaware of her distress as his eyes raked her from head to foot. 'What the blazes...?' He swallowed, his head turning slowly from side to side as if he couldn't believe his eyes.

'I tried to phone you at the office, but it was late and there was no answer.' She tried to excuse her rashness. 'I'd no intention of intruding if you'd made other plans...'

'I decided to treat myself to a shave at the barber's instead of using an electric razor,' he offered, presumably as the reason for his phone's having remained unanswered, closing the distance between them and taking her carrier from her nerveless hand.

Now she was so close to him that she could appreciate the smooth olive glow of his slightly scented skin, from which his customary five o'clock shadow had been professionally removed. It was all she could do not to touch that lean cheek with her fingertips.

'Do I take it you changed your mind about dining with us tonight?' he asked her softly.

'I—yes.' She searched the sparkling sage eyes for an intimation of his reaction. 'If it's not too late, and you still want me?' Her voice quavered a little. This was more of an ordeal than she'd anticipated. How stupid she'd feel if he sent her packing.

'Why, Sapphy?'

She stared at him with startled eyes. There was no way she could tell him the truth—''Because, despite everything I've said and done, I've just discovered that I still love you, and I want you to be successful even if I can't share that success with you...'' Somehow, she had to salvage what was left of her pride, and inspiration came to her aid.

She gave a tiny shrug of her shoulders. 'I got to thinking that one good turn deserves another. You'd promised to show my work to Andreas Constanidou...'

'And you thought I wouldn't unless you did what I asked of you?' His words were gentle enough, but the scowl which accompanied them sounded a warning which made the hairs on the back of her neck prickle.

'Something like that,' she agreed artlessly, smiling in an attempt to resurrect his good humour. 'It seemed a good exchange—but if arrangements have been altered...'

'No,' he assured her roughly. 'The arrangements stand. I was leaving it to the last minute to apologise for your

absence. Wait a moment, let's get rid of your luggage.'
He seized her left hand as if she might disappear if he
left her alone for a moment, taking her with him to the
desk, where he handed over the carrier with instructions
for it to be placed alongside his briefcase.

'Well!' he mused, leading her towards the bar, but
pausing just on the threshold and drawing her to one
side. 'This is a surprise, Sapphy; I'd no idea you were
so amenable to blackmail. Perhaps I should have tried
it earlier in our relationship.'

'Don't!' Hurt, she tried to withdraw her hand from
his clasp, only to find that it held even tighter.

'And this is another surprise, *agape mou*.' He lifted
her hand, palm downward so that the band of rings
sparkled under the light. 'I imagined you'd thrown these
away! It seems your sense of cupidity was greater than
your dislike of me.'

If she hadn't always seen him as invincible, Sapphy
would have supposed that Thane was hurting. But that
speculative glint in his bright eyes must arise from his
desire to wound her rather than from any inner pain of
his own, as must his contemptuous use of a loving epi-
thet. She'd been wrong to suggest that he was black-
mailing her. Thane had never stooped to anything as
base as that, and she would never have accused him of
such if it hadn't been in an effort to protect her own
tender sensibilities. Too late now to apologise or explain. Her reasons for self-preservation were still as valid
as ever.

'They're beautiful rings,' she said quietly, refusing to
show her hurt. 'One day, your daughter may enjoy
wearing them. I wore them tonight because I thought it
would be expected of me. I imagine you've given the
Robinsons the impression that we're happily married,
haven't you?'

'They're certainly under the impression that I love you,' he returned equably. 'It will be up to you to demonstrate whether you reciprocate the feeling or not.' He gave her his tigerish smile, all soft pussycat hiding the killer instinct. 'Do you know, Sapphy, I don't believe you ever thanked me for the eternity ring?'

He made it into a question, but he knew he was right. So did she, to her eternal shame. It was too easy to make an excuse of her illness and the trauma she'd undergone. They hadn't helped matters, but she'd been a selfish, spoilt little girl, demanding that her husband act as she wanted him to, unable to read his emotional response to her in his own actions. She'd taken the ring, thrusting it into her jewellery box with never a word of appreciation, and that had been unforgivable, whatever the circumstances.

Shame and regret brought a flush of mortification to her pearly complexion. 'You made a rotten choice for a wife,' she whispered, unable to meet his chiding gaze. 'But then, that's not news to you.'

'Hmm...' It was a low noise in his throat, almost, but not quite, laughter. 'Reparation wipes out a lot of sins. Now I *do* remember you thanking me for your postdated engagement ring. A similar show of gratitude would be quite acceptable. Not only would it serve as a penance but it would set the tone for the evening, *ne*?'

If his meaning had struck her a moment sooner she could have foiled him, but she made the mistake of pausing to recall just how she had thanked him for the ruby cluster. By the time she'd remembered, it was too late.

Thane had, quite simply, drawn her close into his arms, taken her chin in one firm hand to steady it and possessed her mouth with purpose and authority. They were in a public place and Thane was no exhibitionist, preferring to keep the excesses of emotional display for a place and time where there was no audience, but within the limitations of his own good taste he shook Sapphira to the depths of her spirit.

Rocking back on her high-heels as he deepened the kiss to a loverlike intensity, she was forced to grab at his shoulders to support herself, her fingers digging into his flesh through the light suiting. His body was in intimate contact with her own, his thighs a heavy pressure against the soft silk of her skirt. His hands, splayed against her back, moved with leisurely appreciation, the thumbs caressing the column of her spine.

It was a punishing kiss. Not because he hurt her physically, because he hadn't. He'd taken what she was prepared to give, begged for more and taken that when she hadn't been able to find the willpower to deny him. It had been punishing because he had been demonstrating his superior lust for life, his superior powers of survival. He had kissed her, not because he cared for her, but because he didn't.

Sapphira was gasping when he released her, shocked by her own response and the very real sense of loss she'd experienced when she'd felt his body withdraw from her own. Determined to keep a positive role in the game he was playing, she held up her hand as he would have led her into the bar.

'Wait!' He stopped, eyebrows raised at her peremptory tone. 'That shade of lipstick doesn't suit you!'

The warm curves of his mouth bore no trace of red, but that was beside the point. Taking a tissue from her bag, Sapphira dabbed at his lips, smiling sweetly, with all the proprietorial air of a devoted wife, reducing him to temporary helplessness beneath her touch.

So intent was she on following the sweet, sensuous curve of his mouth that she was unaware that they'd been joined from the other side of the bar entrance by a couple who were regarding her actions with amused tolerance, until Thane took her wrist and twisted her gently round, drawing her into his side and holding her to him by encircling her waist with his muscular arm. Then she heard his pleasantly modulated voice, with its touch of Greek accent that could still wring pleasure from her heart, saying, 'Ah, Philip and Catherine! May I introduce my wife—Sapphira.'

CHAPTER TEN

IT WASN'T an auspicious start to the evening as far as Sapphira was concerned. Still disturbed and confused by Thane's unexpected kiss, she had to draw on all her inner reserves to present a bland face to her hosts. Dear God, she prayed silently, what an impossible situation it was for both of them. Let this evening end amicably and she'd never repeat it, never!

'Of course, we could have dined in our suite.' It was Catherine, addressing her in conspiratorial tones. 'But we would have had to suffer plans and print-outs interfering with the courses, not to mention a hi-tech verbal accompaniment to the dessert course!'

Across the table from her, Philip Robinson smiled, his grey eyes showing genuine amusement as he acknowledged his wife's accusation with a helpless gesture of his hands. 'Be honest, my love. It wasn't just that, was it? Admit it, you're a flower who doesn't enjoy blooming unseen!'

'It is a nice dress, isn't it?' Catherine retorted complacently, running a hand over the gold-threaded black chiffon garment which graced her elegant form, and offering her husband a cheeky grin. 'And it would have been nothing short of criminal to have deprived the tired Greek businessmen enjoying a refreshing drink here in the bar of the sight of Sapphira. I wouldn't like to count the number of heads which have turned in *her* direction since we entered!' Her mouth curved with laughter as she turned her attention to Thane. 'Your countrymen are such true appreciators of feminine beauty, it must make your women feel very special.'

'We certainly have a reputation for showing curiosity,' Thane answered easily, acknowledging the arrival of the drink he'd ordered with a dip of his head. 'In Greece, it's considered only natural to stand and stare if something takes our attention. As far as Sapphira is concerned, as long as the admiration is given from a safe distance, I can tolerate it.'

'Spoken like a true Continental!' Catherine enthused, her dark eyes sparkling with a mischief that made her look nearer Sapphira's age than the mid-forties the latter had guessed her to be at first sight. 'Why is it, I wonder, that Englishmen don't feel the same way about their women—that a beautifully presented wife who can turn heads adds to their own stature?'

'Probably because the women's lobby would be after them, brandishing knives!' Philip Robinson retorted drily. 'It's no longer socially acceptable for a woman to be regarded as a fashion accessory to a man. What do you think, Sapphira?'

'Me?' She'd been following the interchange of ideas with interest, sipping at the glass of dry white wine she'd ordered, feeling her nerves begin to settle under the Robinsons' easy familiarity. Underneath Philip's athletic build and consummate air of authority she detected a warm nature which, with his wife's friendliness, would surely make the evening a success.

'Uh-huh.' Philip regarded her challengingly. 'Do you see yourself as one of Thanos's accessories, a small but important aspect of the way other people see him?'

A quick glance across the table to where Thane sat eyeing her contemplatively offered her no help. Of course, it was only a fun question, but it would be too easy to sow the answer with bitterness, to humiliate him with some caustic comment as she recognised, to her shame, she might have done in those dreadful days of the past. No, what was needed was something glib and light. Something which would keep the spirit of the evening alive.

'Well, Sapphy, how *do* you see me?' His eyes challenged her across the table as he prompted her answer, deliberately exposing himself to the scorn of which he knew her to be capable.

'That's a difficult one to answer,' she murmured, playing for time. 'I must admit, I've never tried to analyse the status quo before, but on consideration I'd say it was fifty-fifty. Half the time when you're centre stage then, yes, I supply the backdrop. The other half, when it's *my* turn to perform, well...' Two entrancing dimples dented her cheeks at the corner of her mouth as her blue eyes taunted him across the glass top of the table. 'Let's just say it wasn't just your brains I married you for. A beautiful man in attendance does more for most women than a facelift!'

'Well said!' Catherine applauded her roundly. 'I think mutual congratulations are in order, don't you? We both seem to have chosen our major accessories with impeccable taste!'

As she accepted the cool clasp of Catherine's hand, Sapphira heard Philip's low laughter.

'I guess you asked for that one, my friend. Still, it's nice to know our womenfolk appreciate us.'

'Yes, isn't it?' Smooth as silk, Thane agreed, but there was no answering smile in his eyes or on his lips as he lifted his glass and drank deeply.

The light exchange at the bar set the mood for the ensuing dinner. Philip Robinson was undoubtedly high-powered in his business life, but he carried no pretensions into his off-duty time. The meal progressed in an

ambience of easy camaraderie, Catherine showing particular interest in Victoria and Stephanos, drawing
Sapphira out to talk about them, encouraging the recital
of various amusing stories.

'Our daughter is twenty,' Catherine confided towards
the end of the meal, helping herself to a *petit four*. 'She's
determined not to marry or have a family until she's well-
established in a career, so I shall have a long time to
wait before achieving that happy status where one can
enjoy young children without all the hassle of having
them with one all the time! Frankly, I can't imagine how
you cope with twins when they're tiny!'

'I was lucky,' Sapphira admitted, astounded to find
that she believed what she was saying. 'We had a housekeeper, and Thane engaged a nursery nurse. He—he did
everything possible to make life easy for me.' Despite
her resolve her voice broke slightly.

'But it was still a strain, hmm?' Catherine regarded
her with knowing, compassionate eyes. 'Still, the best is
yet to come, isn't it: the joy of seeing them go to school,
of being able to communicate with them as they grow
older, of helping and guiding them...?'

All the things she might never do, at least not as the
primary influence in their lives! With a strangled gasp,
Sapphira pushed back her chair.

'Yes,' she managed to answer Catherine's question,
before flicking a quick glance round the table. 'Will you
please excuse me a moment?'

Subsiding on a chair in the powder-room, she pulled
herself together. Having agreed to play the part re-
quested of her, she was honour-bound to see it through
with good grace. A few moments spent on renewing her
make-up and drinking a glass of ice-cool water, and she
was ready to pin a polite smile to her trembling mouth
and walk back to the restaurant.

Thane was waiting for her just before the entrance,
taking her arm and drawing her gently to one side as she
raised questioning eyes to his set face.

'What's the matter? Is something wrong?'

'That's the question I want to ask you, Sapphy.' He
looked grim. 'You seemed upset when you left the table.
Is this all proving too much for you?'

'No, not at all. I didn't mean to appear rude. Were
the Robinsons offended?'

'No.' He put her fears at rest. 'Perhaps it's just me,
over-reacting. I was concerned in case you'd decided to
make a dash for home.'

'That would have been embarrassing for you to explain away!' She smiled faintly. 'No, it's just I feel a
little under-rehearsed in the part I'm playing.' Unconsciously, her hands stroked the silk of her two-piece,
smoothing the extended bodice over her hips.

'And not entirely at ease with your new costume either,
hmm?' His sharp eyes hadn't missed the nervous gesture,
gleaming with an odd light which she couldn't decipher.

'It doesn't suit me?' All her insecurity was in the
question and she could have bitten her tongue out once
she'd spoken. The last thing she'd wanted to do was
betray her inadequacies to her self-assured escort.

'Oh, it suits you, Sapphy.' The sparkle in his eyes
deepened, the dimness of the light dilating his pupils so
it was like gazing into pools of infinite depths. 'What
made you choose that colour, I wonder?'

'No special reason.' She considered the question
seriously, surprised that Thane should question her on
it. 'I suppose I thought it would give me confidence.
One can't hide in a corner when one's wearing scarlet!'
She gave a nervous laugh.

'Not because it was the colour of your wedding dress?'

'No!' Shocked by the quiet intensity of his rapid question, Sapphy denied the allegation instantly. She hadn't, had she? Or had Angelia's reference to that photograph on Thane's desk started off a subconscious train of thought which had led her inexorably to that boutique? 'Why should I do that?' she asked defensively.

'I don't know.' His narrowed gaze glittered over her. 'Why should you cut off your hair?'

'You object?' It was a long time since he'd shown any interest in her personal appearance, and her pulse quickened alarmingly, sensing his disapproval. Wearily she accorded that his opinion shouldn't matter; the painful truth was that it still did.

'I don't have any right to object, do I?' he asked smoothly, standing so close to her that she felt over-powered by his presence. 'But since you request my opinion, I have to say...' He paused, deliberately pro-longing the torture, allowing his regard to dwell, unfet-tered, not only on her new hairstyle, but on the flushed face it framed. 'I don't think I've ever seen you looking more beautiful—even on our wedding day.'

'Oh!' The unstinted compliment had taken her by sur-prise, sending a spurt of pure pleasure zinging through her, until she remembered that it was in Thane's interests to keep her sweet. Making a quick recovery, she raised her eyebrows, apeing amusement. 'How very *gallant* of you, Thane. Shall we rejoin the Robinsons?'

'Of course.' His dark head inclined slightly as, moving forward, he opened the doors to the restaurant for her, one hand splayed lightly against her waist, guiding her forward with the intimate touch of one who had the right of possession.

Instinctively Sapphira's back tensed against the pressure of his palm as he smiled down at her. 'The Robinsons have invited us back to their suite for more coffee and liqueurs. I take it you have no objection? Philip has an exciting concept he wants to discuss with me before he returns to England.'

Sapphira could hear the excitement curdling the depths of his husky voice and sensed, behind the nonchalance of his statement, the importance of the proposed discussion.

'I'll stay with you as long as you need me,' she said quietly.

Her assurance was greeted by a low laugh. 'Why, Sapphy, what a rash undertaking.' His mocking glance ridiculed her, but he denied her the satisfaction of re-phrasing her answer, adding abruptly. 'I'll have to phone Ephimi and tell her we may be very late.'

'She doesn't know we're together, Thane.'

'Then she'll be delighted to learn that we are, won't she?' His voice had an edge to it as his green eyes flared darkly. Sapphira drew in a sharp breath as his arm curled possessively round her shoulders on their approach to their table.

She stole a quick, almost guilty glance at his profile. He looked just as he had the first time she'd set eyes on him; aloof, unemotional, arrogantly sure of himself and possessing a devious, charming beauty.

'Sapphy and I would be delighted to extend the evening further, as you suggested,' he told their hosts pleasantly.

The Robinsons' suite proved as luxurious as one would expect in a first-class hotel. With the men involved in complicated design problems, Sapphira settled down to continue her conversation with Catherine, Philip Robinson's wife proving to be an amusing and stimu-lating companion. As the evening lengthened into night, the two women found plenty of interests in common, ranging from shared tastes in music and drama, a creative talent for cooking and even a mutual acquaintance in Sapphira's old headmaster.

Sapphira was only aware that Thane had used the telephone when he called her name softly across the room at a break in her exchange of reminiscences with Catherine.

'Yes, darling?' She wasn't even aware that she'd used an endearment until she saw Thane raise one lazy eyebrow in acknowledgement of her slip. Relaxed and happy, living in a comfortable dream, she had allowed her defences to crumble. Well, she could hardly apologise for using the word, could she? She'd just have to brazen it out. Trying to look unconcerned, she met the ironic gleam in his eyes with a blank stare.

'I'm afraid I didn't realise how late it was getting, *mahtia mou.*' He paid her back in her own coin. 'If we go home now, we're going to disturb the whole household, so I've booked us in here for the night.' He stood looking at her, his jacket long since discarded, his tie askew, shirt open at the neck, his hair curling disarmingly over his forehead, the dark shadow beginning to grace his chin giving him a rakish, piratical air, inviting her comment.

'Oh, but...' Totally unprepared for such a circumstance, Sapphira found it impossible to get her thoughts in order.

'Don't worry, the receptionist is going to speak to the housekeeper's department. She assures me they will be able to supply us with toothbrushes and an electric razor for me, and all rooms automatically have the basic toilet requisites. I'm sure we can manage for one night.'

'I'm sure we can,' she found herself saying. There was a lot of sense in the arrangement. Thane's elegantly boned face seemed a little drawn, and there was a tiredness behind the sparkle of his malachite eyes that touched her heart.

By the time they'd said goodnight to their hosts, and Thane had collected the key and her carrier from reception, another half-hour had passed. She was standing behind him as he opened the door to their room, smothering a yawn with the palm of her hand, when she heard him utter what could only be an expletive in his own language.

'What is it?' She squeezed past him into the room, imagining all kinds of disaster, but the sight which met her eyes was gracious and appealing. The room was large, furnished with modern, attractive furniture including a comfortable-looking armchair and writing desk and chair. There was even a bowl of fruit on a low table and a vase of flowers on the dressing-table. Then she saw the reason for his ill-tempered oath.

'Oh!' She gazed blankly at the large double-bed.

'You have to believe me, Sapphy,' he said savagely. 'I didn't plan this. I did ask for a double room, it's true, but, as you know, most hotel rooms in Greece have two beds in a room. Since I could hardly ask for two single rooms, I thought that arrangement would be acceptable in the circumstances.'

'I think it must be the bridal suite,' she offered serenely, amused by his furious reaction, and finding herself strangely unable to treat the matter half as seriously: perhaps it was because she was tired; perhaps simply because the whole evening had recaptured something of the past which she regretted losing.

Walking gracefully across the room, she opened the door to the bathroom.

'It's very luxurious,' she called back over her shoulder. 'Two hand-basins and lots of gold plating. I'm afraid the bath is a little small for you to spend the night in, though!'

'I'll sleep in the chair.' He walked across and flung his long body down into it. 'You have the bathroom first. I'll go in when you've finished.' Eyes closed, lashes shadowing his cheekbones, he slumped down. 'Be as quick as you can, won't you?'

She obeyed him without demur, stripping off in the bathroom for the quickest of quick showers before towelling herself down and replacing the scarlet body-shaper, trying to stop her mind from dwelling on the days when she and Thane had shared a bathroom, and the sheer pleasure she had taken in watching him beneath the shower.

Whereas she was content to pamper her skin, Thane had always scrubbed and stimulated his lean golden body with a vigour which was typically masculine, as if he'd wanted to scrub off the accumulated dirt of years. Somehow, the towels she'd used were only mildly damp afterwards, whereas Thane's were, inevitably, soaked. How she missed those sopping towels...

She couldn't go out into the bedroom clad only like this. She assessed herself quickly, but thoroughly, in the full-length mirror, taking the first opportunity to see the body-shaper *in situ*. Good heavens! Was this really her? Fascinated by the image she saw, Sapphira touched her proudly rounded breasts with wondering fingers.

Beneath the deep panel of lace which extended to her navel, her skin gleamed with a pearly lustre. And her legs! The garment was cut flatteringly high, making them appear endless, the lower part of her hips and loins masked only by the stretch lace. Not unusually vain, she knew she was looking at the girl she had once been, and felt a spurt of very feminine pleasure.

Quickly seizing a large unused towel she tied it, sarong-style, beneath her arms and re-entered the bedroom.

Thane was where she'd left him, looking more uncomfortable than ever. The back of the chair only reached his shoulder blades, so there was no place for him to rest his head. Only a masochist would have chosen to spend the night there. Only a sadist would have allowed him to do so.

'The bathroom's free, Thane.' She spoke softly, sure he couldn't possibly be asleep in such uncomfortable circumstances. 'Look, there's no reason why we can't share the same bed,' she continued reasonably, keeping her voice unemotional. 'It's quite large. I accept that you didn't arrange this purposely. In the circumstances, it seems the sensible thing to do.'

'That's very charitable of you, Sapphy.' He regarded her from behind heavy eyelids, his reaction unreadable. 'I'll bear it in mind.'

'Good!' She slipped beneath the sheet before unwrapping her towel and throwing it out on to the floor. 'Sleep well, then!'

She was aware that he'd risen to his feet and made for the bathroom. In a few minutes she would feel his weight on the bed beside her. Why should the prospect excite her? It was part of the fantasy which she'd gradually been building up over the evening, encouraged by good food, good wine and good company. It had been so easy in that atmosphere of self-indulgence to fool herself into believing that they were the ideal couple they were pretending to be: in love with each other and with two adorable children to complete the family circle. Was it so wrong to extend the illusion for a few more hours? Surely not, if she was strong enough to face reality when morning light arrived.

Tense and expectant, she lay there, breathing quietly, every cell of her body awake now for the moment when she would sense Thane's body beside her own. From then on, she could indulge her own imagination until she fell asleep, satiated with the thoughts of what might have been.

She heard the slight movement of the bathroom door, saw the jagged flare of light before he flicked the switch, and sensed his approach as every nerve in her body tingled with suspenseful anticipation. Then there was nothing. Just a long, stretching silence and an empty bed beside her.

'Thane?' She reached for the low-watt bedside lamp. He was still dressed in shirt and trousers, spread-eagled uncomfortably in the armchair, his head propped up on his hand. 'Thane!' she repeated his name sharply.

When there was still no reply she uttered a sigh of exasperation, scrambling out of bed and taking the few steps necessary to stand in front of him. 'Thane!' She shook his shoulder, saw his eyelids flicker and a muscle twitch beneath his cheekbone. 'What are you doing? We agreed you should share the bed!'

'We agreed nothing of the kind!' he barked irritably. 'I said I'd bear it in mind, which I did, before rejecting it. For God's sake, go back to bed, Sapphy, and let me find peace in my own way!'

'But this is absurd!' She stood, legs astride, hands on hips, totally oblivious of how she must appear to the sleepy-eyed man in the chair before her: angry because she hated to see him so uncomfortable, frustrated because he was denying her her harmless fantasy, puzzled because she couldn't understand his reluctance. 'Do you think I'm going to seduce you?' she demanded furiously, all her pent-up emotion lending a shrill edge of accusation to her voice.

'No.' He uncurled his long body, taking her by surprise as he rose to his full height, a dominating figure, power emanating from every pulse-beat that throbbed through his lean frame. 'No, Sapphy,' he repeated more gently. 'It's because I'm very much afraid I might seduce you.'

It was so unexpected that she could only stand where she was and gasp.

'You think I'm lying?' His every attitude was dangerous, his body poised for action, some undercurrent of vitality surging through his veins so that his sleepiness became only an illusion.

She could have moved, but she chose not to. Even when his arms reached for her she put up no resistance. Even when he pulled her close to his hard frame she made no effort to fight him, and when his hands travelled over the silk and lace of the only garment she wore, moulding her body with a sureness of touch that awakened the slumbering fires of her metabolism, she could only give a shiver of delight and hold up her mouth for the deep possession of his kiss.

He was trembling. Not overtly, but deep inside, so that being close to him was like being in contact with a mighty generator thrumming away internally. Her arms linked behind his neck, drawing his head down in intimate contact, while her mouth opened to receive his homage. It seemed so right, as if it had been ordained from the beginning of the evening, that when he finally released her the sense of loss she experienced was devastating.

'Now do you see why I won't share your bed?' he asked tautly, his voice hoarse, the words disjointed. 'Leave me alone or I won't be responsible for the consequences. Do you understand?'

'Yes.' He could hardly have made his point more clearly, but still she didn't move. Instead she moistened her dry lips with the tip of her tongue, fully aware that his eyes, dark-pupilled and glazed with the glow of sexual arousal, were following the small manoeuvre. 'I—I won't be able to sleep, thinking of you trying to relax in that chair.'

'Ten seconds, Sapphy.' He spoke with an effort. 'I'll give you ten seconds to get back into bed and turn out the light, otherwise...'

She counted to ten under her breath, not moving a muscle, watching his laboured breathing, knowing exactly what she was inviting and revelling in it. Why not live out her fantasy to its extreme? One last night—if not of mutual love—then of the nearest thing she could equate to it! One last memory to take with her into the limbo which awaited her.

When Thane lifted her effortlessly, depositing her on the bed and plunging the room into darkness, her hands reached for him, threading between the open edges of his shirt, touching his muscled chest with fingers primed with sweet remembrance. She heard his groan of acceptance and grew bolder, her palms travelling downwards to caress the smooth planes of his abdomen beneath the loosened waistband of his trousers. Once more, just once more...

She heard the rasp of his breath, and knew when he drew away from her that it was in order to make her task easier. When he rolled back into her arms he was naked. Time was encapsulated as she reached for him once more, knowing fingers renewing their lost acquaintance, as his flesh quickened beneath their caress.

Once again she was young and carefree, experiencing the supreme physical joys of loving and being loved, lost in a world of sensual pleasure, as Thane returned her caresses, lowering the thin straps of her body-shaper to expose the tender swelling of her opalescent breasts, kissing their damask tips with a gentle homage which acknowledged their state of increased sensitivity.

Their bodies reached for each other, no strangers to the other's needs, their responses heightened by the lapse of time which had denied their pleasure. Only when Thane slid the scarlet garment down beneath her waist did Sapphira stiffen in terrified anticipation of the disgust he had manifested the last time they had lain together, only to relax with a sigh of relief as she realised that the darkness would hide her disfigurement and the slender silver scar would be imperceptible to his exploring fingers.

When he spoke to her with his hands and mouth, with sighs and little gasps of pleasure, she answered him with murmurs and whimpers, encouraging and enticing him with a responsive elation which had lain dormant for so long. It was not going to be long before the time was right for the ultimate fulfilment, as heated skin fired heated skin, encouraging the raging flames of desire to burn to their brightest.

When Thane gasped out her name, as if in agony— 'Sapphy!'—she curled up beneath him, offering herself with a generous sweetness which asked nothing in return save the gift of himself, drawing him into her velvet fastness, exulting when he moaned his pleasure and his pain, jubilant when he cried out in the wild triumph of orgasm.

Like Samson sheared by Delilah, he lay against her, totally vulnerable, unable to move a muscle in the aftermath of passion and her hands reached intuitively to protect his defencelessness, one palm protecting the tender nape of his neck, the other closing against his back as if it were threatened by some savage's arrow.

The fantasy was nearly complete. Now she had until
the morning before her dream ended. As he stirred and
turned on his back, she rested her head against his still-
heaving chest, hearing the strength of his steady heartbeat
echoing her own. She felt more alive than she had in
years, as if Thane's passion had instilled in her some of
his own vitality, lighting internal fires which fed their
warmth through every part of her system.

When she awakened later that morning she was alone
in bed. It took her a few moments to recapture the events
of the previous night, and a few more moments to decide
that she had no regrets. There was no longer any point
in denying to herself that she still loved Thane. The
realisation had come too late to repair the damage she
had caused in the past, but at least she was no longer
lying to herself.

'Ah, you're awake.' The object of her musing emerged
from the bathroom fully dressed, his face stern and
drawn. 'I'll see you downstairs in the dining-room for
breakfast. Don't be too long, will you? The sooner we
get back to Andromeda, the better.'

Swallowing hard in an attempt to disperse the sudden
lump which appeared to have formed in her throat,
Sapphira nodded her head as without a further word
Thane left the bedroom.

What had she hoped for? Fighting down her disappointment, she swung her bare legs from the bed. At
least he'd behaved with discretion, leaving the bedroom
so she could move freely in her nakedness. She had never
believed he would greet her with the same passion the
morning after. Thane was a virile man, his body as easily
aroused as any male animal's in the presence of a nubile
female, and she had encouraged him against his will.

Stumbling towards the bathroom, she refused to make
any excuses for herself. She'd repeated her folly of the

past, making herself available to a transitory need. Thane had paid dearly for her first indiscretion. One look at his hard face that morning and she knew he was furious that he'd succumbed to her unwelcome invitation.

Speedily she showered and dressed herself in her street clothes of yesterday, bundling the shameful scarlet lingerie into the carrier alongside the new dress, folded neatly but without enthusiasm. All she had accomplished was to make him detest her more than ever, yet even now she couldn't bring herself to regret what had happened: not with the lingering sensation of his possession a hot ache inside her.

Breakfast was a silent meal, as was the car journey which succeeded it. Arriving at the villa, Thane opened the front door, standing back to allow her to enter first, as Ephimi came down the hallway to greet them with a smile.

'How are the *didimee*?' Sapphira asked instantly, reassured by the older woman's obvious complacency.

'As lively as ever,' Ephimi confirmed. 'As is Tigris!'

'I'll go up and see them...'

'In a moment!' Thane seized her arm, restraining her as she would have mounted the stairs. 'I need to speak with you first in private. Come into the study, will you, please?'

Now what? A post-mortem? Recriminations? She wished with all her heart that she could find the courage to refuse the invitation, which was only an order in disguise. Better by far that what had happened last night between them be simply forgotten. Erased for ever, like the fantasy it had been. To analyse what had happened would degrade it and that was something she couldn't bear.

'Must we?' Her blue eyes beseeched him for understanding. 'There isn't really anything to say.'

'You're wrong, Sapphy.' He sounded sad as he ushered her into the study, closing the door behind him and indicating that she sit in one of the armchairs as he paced the floor in front of her. 'I have something very important to say to you.'

'Yes?' Her chest felt tight, as if the bones were crushing inwards, making it painful to breathe, forcing her heart to increase its pace.

'You were right when you said we couldn't live like this.' He stopped prowling to stand in front of her, staring down at her like a judge about to pronounce sentence. 'I've changed my mind, Sapphy. I'll do everything I can to make it easy for you to divorce me.'

CHAPTER ELEVEN

THANE'S words struck her like a body blow, depriving her of the power to speak, only her eyes flexing open in shock and her rapidly fading colour betraying her distress.

'I was a fool to believe a separation would work.' He delivered the harsh verdict bleakly. 'You were right from the start—divorce is the only answer. It was madness on my part to think I could tether you to my side forever.'

'And the children?' It was little more than a whisper. She had handed over her joint custody on the implicit understanding that she would always be able to be near them. Was he going to use her gesture against her in divorce proceedings?

'Will remain in your care, naturally.' His jaw tightened as his teeth clenched in a momentary reaction to keep control. 'After last night I could hardly claim to be a man of integrity or honour!'

He was hurting badly, flailing himself with scorn because he had corrupted his *philotimo*. In his own estimation, he was disgraced, and the knowledge was tormenting him.

Sapphira's initial relief at his words was tempered with a mixture of other emotions: compassion for his pain, indignation that he might suspect her of manipulating him for her own purposes, and an aching guilt that she had been responsible for everything that had happened between them earlier that morning.

'You think I would use that against you in a court of law?' she asked proudly. 'Do you think I really have so

173

little sensibility—or perhaps you think I planned the whole thing to steal the children from you?' Her voice shook.

'When it was I who booked the room?' He gave a bitter laugh. 'No, Sapphy, I don't suspect you of any devious plot. Do you think I don't know you were the injured innocent?'

Injured—yes, but not the way he supposed; innocent—oh, no. She hadn't been that. Puzzled, she stared up at his rigidly held body.

'I—I can understand why you've changed your mind about a divorce.' What future was there for a man of Thane's warmth and vitality tied to a woman he couldn't love? 'But you told me once that you'd never give up your son.'

'Yes.' He swallowed deeply. 'That was before you made your own sacrifice and showed me how unselfish love truly is: that, however deeply one is involved, when the time comes to let go it has to be done with grace and style, no matter how agonising the heartbreak.

'You were right when you said that Stephanos and Victoria needed each other, but that's not all. However much I want to, I can't give them a mother's love and attention. It's not just that I'm out of the house for most of the time—it's a lot more: things I can't even begin to quantify. I tried to shut my eyes to my own deficiencies, but after the holiday, when you went back to your new apartment, they were impossible to hide from. Stephanos's trauma was only the tip of the iceberg.'

He paused, while Sapphira struggled to assimilate what he was saying.

'So you see...' He gave her a sad, twisted smile that didn't touch his eyes. 'Now you've awakened me to the children's needs, I have no option but to ignore my own yearnings and stand down in your favour. I don't deny that it will hurt, but it's no more than I deserve. From the very start I made your life a misery—seducing you, bringing you miles away from your friends and family, settling you in a country whose language you were unfamiliar with, making you pregnant within such a short time of our marriage...' his breath sawed in his chest '...then when you were ill I didn't even recognise the symptoms. I lacked patience and understanding...*Theos mou*, Sapphy! You had every right to expect total support from me—and I gave you nothing! I deserve all the loathing you feel for me.'

'It wasn't your fault, Thane!' The need to share his guilt was overwhelming. 'I was self-centred and immature. I didn't even try to share your life.' Unable to meet his eyes, she stared down at her hands. 'Besides, it was *I* who seduced *you*. I threw myself at you without any thought of the consequences. Even when you told my brother we were going to be married I fooled myself into believing that it was because you loved me, ignoring the obvious reason—that you had been the victim of a passing fancy, and felt honour-bound to "make an honest woman of me" after we were discovered as we were.'

His soft laugh took her by surprise, causing her to raise her head. 'Darling Sapphy! Of course I loved you! I was never so green as to allow myself to be seduced against my will. If I hadn't had every intention of marrying you I would never have got into a situation which was inherently compromising. Your charming and flattering reaction to me only made my plans mature faster than I could have dared to hope for.'

'You loved me?' For years she had persuaded herself that it was untrue. Now, of all times, he surely wouldn't lie?

'Of course I did.' His pensive gaze caressed her. 'Have you forgotten our first year together?'

'No, of course I haven't!' Her eyes dropped from his face, fastening somewhere in the centre of his chest where the sunlight caught the reflection of a pearlised button on his shirt. 'But I destroyed it all, didn't I? I was spoilt and temperamental, demanding and cruel. I killed everything that might have flourished between us.'

'You were ill, Sapphy! And, fool that I was, I didn't recognise it. *Theos mou!* What you suffered both before and after our twins were born! The truth was, I was too jealous to see it. I wasn't prepared to share you—even with our children. Oh, I loved all three of you, but it was you I wanted most. I felt rejected when you spent every day and night with them.

'I couldn't understand why you were so obsessed with them. All my sisters had had children but they'd never reacted so strongly...Sapphy, are you listening?' He dropped down on one knee beside her chair, touching her hand with gentle fingers. 'It was only when in desperation I asked Abby to visit us that I began to understand. I'd hoped that she might be able to get through to you—to open up a channel of communication between us. It was Abby who made me see that my sisters had been surrounded by large families—grandmothers, aunts, cousins, et cetera—someone always there to take responsibility to share the load, while you had had nobody of your own race or family. Until then, I'd been arrogant enough to assume that I could provide all the support you needed, but because of the demands of my business I was seldom there when you wanted me, and I was too blind to see it.' He made a helpless gesture with his hands. 'I wasn't a poor man, but I had to guarantee the source of my income.' A wry smile twisted his mouth. 'Two more little mouths to feed and that was without taking into consideration Spiridoula's wages.'

'And all you got for your trouble was a screaming, hysterical wife who accused you of having an affair with her sister.' Her gaze strayed to the lean capable fingers that rested on her hand. She'd thrown so much away. Yet talking about it was strangely therapeutic, like pouring antiseptic on a wound: painful at first, but necessary, because the healing process would follow. 'If I'd been more rational at the time I would never have made such a wild accusation...' Despite a massive effort of self-control, two teardrops overflowed and ran down her cheeks.

'Don't cry, Sapphy.' Gently, Thane raised a finger and absorbed the tiny drops. 'You weren't responsible for your actions; your whole metabolism was in disorder.'

'But afterwards, when I came back from the clinic, it wasn't,' she accused herself pitilessly. 'I was just full of self-pity. Instead of looking towards the future, all I kept asking myself was, why had it happened to me? Instead of being delighted that I'd been totally cured, all I could think of was how unfortunate I'd been. I was a whining misery of a spoilt brat that no man could have tolerated.'

'There's never been another woman, Sapphy,' he said sadly. 'The most Angelia Andronicos ever was was a steadfast friend and an efficient, helpful business colleague.'

'I know,' she whispered. 'She came to see me yesterday and said the same thing, but I was already beginning to realise, even before then, that I believed it because I wanted to, because it gave me someone else to blame for my own inadequacies, because it was the punishment I deserved for the way I'd treated you. But these last few weeks, since the separation order, it's as if I've suddenly grown up. All the kinks and tangles in my mind seem to have got straightened out, and I'm seeing things more clearly than I have for years.'

'Don't blame yourself, *agape mou*.' Neatly Thane fielded two further crystal drops, his forefinger stroking the soft skin of her cheek, his voice deepening with emotion. 'The original fault was mine. I should have seen that what you felt for me at the start was infatuation. It was impossibly arrogant of me to dare to believe you loved me, but I wanted you so badly that I allowed myself to become blinded to reality. Marrying you was one of the most selfish acts I've ever performed in my life. The other one was accepting your sacrifice to hand over our daughter.'

How could she tell him that he was wrong, that he was the only man she had ever loved? How could she tell him *that* when he had just told her he wanted a divorce... when the original passion he had felt for her had been killed by time and neglect?

Sapphira slid her hand away from his touch, finding a tissue tucked into her sleeve and raising it to her eyes to reduce their brimming. And, loving him, how could she accept the sacrifice he was now prepared to make when she knew from personal experience the agony it would cause him?

'Well——' his face was strained, fine lines round his mouth contorting its sweeping lines into a grimace '—there's only one way left to make amends to you, and that's by freeing you to go to a man you are able to love as much as he loves you.'

'There isn't anyone.' Pitifully, her eyes pleaded for him to believe her. 'Michael was no more to me than Angelia to you. That time you saw him kissing me, it was because I'd told him there could never be a future for us in the way he wanted: that we could only ever be friends.'

For five seconds he didn't answer, then he gave a bitter laugh. 'I was jealous of them both, you know—Lorna and Michael—because they were able to give you something that I was incapable of ... consolation.'

'Thane—please.' Her heart a wild drum in her chest, she clasped her hands in unconscious supplication. 'Perhaps it could all have been different if we'd both tried a little harder to work at solving our differences right at the beginning.'

'Hmm!' He gave a humourless laugh. 'I'd give ten years of my life to be able to go back in time and start again, knowing what I know now.'

'Instead, you want a divorce,' she said listlessly, amazed when he shook his dark head.

'No, I didn't say that, Sapphy. What I said was that I'd make it easy for you to get the divorce *you* wanted. That's not the same thing at all. Don't you see? I tried to keep you tied to me. Kept hoping that one day a miracle would happen and I'd be able to awaken your love again. But it never did. Things went from bad to worse until that evening we quarrelled and fought. Suddenly in the midst of all that anger I wanted you so desperately that I began to believe that, if I couldn't reach you with words, I could reach you with actions: that if we became lovers again it would act as a catalyst, that my body would speak to you in sweeter terms than my tongue could find!' Bitterness twisted his mouth.

White-lipped, Sapphira sprang to her feet, hands clenched at her sides.

'But you couldn't go through with it.' Even speaking the words hurt, as she recalled the look of horror on his face as he'd stared at her unclothed body. 'You were repulsed by my ugly body.'

'Sapphy! What are you saying?' He was across the room in two strides, grasping her by her rigid shoulders, forcing her to look at him. 'I was repulsed, yes! But not by you...by myself. I'd been caught up in a maze of passion and desire, tinged with anger and a growing shame I fought against recognising—and then I saw the fine line of your scar. Hardly visible, it's true, but nothing could have reminded me so forcibly of what I'd already made you suffer. I was older than you, more experienced, and I'd selfishly deprived you of your youth and freedom, and here I was compounding those sins, about to bend you once more to my will.' He sighed. 'I've hated myself many times these last few months but seldom as much as I did then.'

'Oh.' She stared at him blankly. 'I thought it was because you found me ugly. I was so thin and dried up...'

He shook his head. 'You'll always be beautiful to me, Sapphy,' he told her with aching simplicity. 'No, it was I who was ugly, but I still wasn't prepared to give you up. That's why, when you fled to Lorna, I suggested a legal separation. I reasoned that you would feel protected from the threat of any physical advance from me but I would still have access to you—and, most importantly of all, you wouldn't be able to marry anyone else. I was convinced I'd terrified you with my unwarranted attack, and the only possible way was to give you plenty of space and time and play the rest by ear. I was going to take things very slowly, try to court you as I should have done at the beginning.'

'And now it's too late.' Despair thickened her voice, as he raised a gentle hand to stroke her cheek.

'You can ask me that after what happened to us last night? Ah, Sapphy...' He touched her silky hair reverently. 'Do you still not understand? I can't trust myself to be near you and not hurt you. After all the trouble you had with the twins I swore to myself that I'd never allow you to become pregnant again; yet last night I loved you with an abandon that took nothing into consideration. If I'd had half the willpower I pride myself on, I would have spent the night downstairs in the bar because I don't go around prepared for casual encounters. They just aren't my style. Instead...' His voice cracked uncontrollably. 'I'm just no good to you, Sapphy. I have to let you go because I love you, and I can't trust myself to keep my distance when you're near me. And I have to let you have our children—because—I love them, too.' He moved, half turning towards his desk, concealing his face from her.

For a moment, shock held her rigid and she thought she might faint from the hard pulse of the artery throbbing in her head. 'You still love me?' A great wave of warmth was born somewhere deep inside her, flowing through her veins, bringing with it a surge of almost unbearable happiness. 'Then—then can't we make a new start?' Her voice shook with a powerful emotion.

Shoulders hunched, Thane walked to the window, staring out of it and presenting her with the tough, powerful outline of his tall frame against the light.

'Continue with our platonic marriage, you mean? No; I thought it might work, but it's impossible. I can't see you without wanting to love you—and I can't love you without hurting you. Neither have I the right to prevent you from finding your own happiness, wherever and with whomever you choose.' He turned to face her, his mouth tilted into a faint smile, but his eyes were tormented. 'It was you who taught me the lesson—that true love cannot be selfish; that there are times when the only honourable action is to have, to hold... and, in time, let go!'

'But I don't want to go!' Sapphira drew in a deep breath, willing him to listen and believe. 'I—I love you, too, Thane! I never stopped loving you, but it was too powerful for me to handle when it got entangled with jealousy and fear, and I couldn't find the way to communicate with you. I suppose I wanted you to know my feelings intuitively. When you didn't, I persuaded myself that I hated you—but it was never true.'

She gave a breathless little laugh as he stood, motionless as a statue, stunned into silence by her powerful attestation; then she continued, her voice shaking with emotion, 'And it's all right about last night. It's the most unlikely time possible to increase our family. In any case, the doctors told me I'd probably not suffer that way again, and even if I did, they'd be ready to treat it before it got out of hand, and . . . and if you hadn't made love to me I would have been devastated because as soon as I saw that double bed my imagination was leaping ahead . . .'

'Dear God,' Thane said piously, at last, 'Please don't let this be a dream!' He held out his arms and she went into them, clinging to his shoulders for strength as her legs weakened, laying her head against his chest and he dipped his dark head to rest on her shoulder while his arms enfolded her possessively. For several seconds they stood there enjoying each other's nearness, their auras mingling in sweet remembrance, their senses sharpening and interacting in a mounting wave of excitement.

When Sapphira felt the unmistakable presence of his physical need for her, she moved enticingly against him, rejoicing in the sound of his half-muffled groan. 'Why don't we go to bed, *agape mou*?' she whispered, feeding his desire with a captivating smile.

'What would Ephimi think?' He pretended to be shocked, but the gleam in his green eyes and his spasmodic inhalation of breath denounced him as a liar.

'We don't pay her to think!' She laughed up into his beloved face and, reading everything there she needed to know, she sighed with infinite satisfaction.

They were the last words she spoke for a long time, as Thane scooped her up in his arms and carried her with surprising speed upstairs into the master bedroom, where, after locking the door, he became once more the man of her dreams and her life—Thane— lord . . . liege . . . master.

'Happy?'

It was the question he had often asked her in the early days, and she gave the old reply, 'Delirious!'

He stirred lethargically, his sleek body naked and un- ashamed in the golden light of the mid-morning. 'We've got a lot of plans to make, Sapphy.'

'Mm . . .' Satiated with contentment and pleasure, she began to trace circles round the small sturdy nipples adorning his muscled chest. 'Such as?'

'Get the separation order quashed for a start!' He grabbed at her hand, stilling it. 'Then, if we get the con- tract from Philip Robinson, and there's an excellent chance we will, especially after the rapport we enjoyed last night, I'll take you and the children with me to England for six months. I can supervise the installation and operation of the programs and you can see your family again.'

'I'd like that.' Sapphira smiled. She owed Abby an abject apology, and nothing would please her more now than to be able to deliver it in person. Miraculously, the threads of her life were growing strong again, her tat- tered loving repaired, clothed in the apparel of under- standing and forgiveness.

He sighed luxuriously, placing a loving hand on one of her tender breasts, caressing it with sure, reverent fingers.

'You know, I really thought I'd lost you for good when you came to me that day and handed over your custody of Vicki.'

'You thought I was about to elope with Michael.' She remembered his hostility, and smiled. 'There was never any chance of that!'

'But I didn't know that then, and I had to speed up all the plans I'd made to bring you back into my life, instead of laying siege to you slowly and gently over several months, proving to you that there was more, much more, to the way I felt about you than the joy of possessing you physically.'

Sapphira smiled, appreciating his strategy. 'Lucky for you that you'd already planned to go to Konstantinos!'

'Oh, but I hadn't!' Mischief sharpened his green eyes. 'Oh, sure, I'd told Stephanos I'd take him to the seaside, but I'd meant somewhere much nearer. But if I was to reawaken pleasant memories—then it had to be Konstantinos, where we were once so happy.'

A sudden suspicion made Sapphira narrow her eyes as she stared down into his complacent face.

'And Spiridoula's boyfriend?'

'Ah, him.' He paused. 'Well, he *is* Greek and I'm sure if he'd been made aware of the circumstances he would have objected, so I simply assumed he already had.'

'You devious——'

'Hush!' He silenced her mouth with a kiss. 'No more maledictions—you remember? Besides, I wasn't the only crafty one. Don't forget, our son had his own plans for bringing you back where you belong. Without his intervention, we probably wouldn't be here now. It would have taken me a lot longer to persuade you to return to Andromeda, although that was what my long-term plan was.'

'But you said you were going to sell it!'

'Did I?' His smile was positively Machiavellian. 'Well, I suppose it might have come to that, but in the short

term I just wanted to rekindle your first feelings for it—
make it more difficult for you keep away from it.'

Obediently Sapphira lapsed into temporary silence,
content just to be close to him, to savour the sweet es-
sences of his body, but there was just one point in the
record that she had to put right.

'You may not believe this, but Lorna will be so happy
for both of us that we've found a happy ending. I know
you resented her, but all she ever wanted was my happiness. In fact she realised even before I did that I was still
in love with you. In her own way, she was as devious as
you were—giving me gifts to take with me to
Konstantinos, which were intended to reawaken my sense
of romance and make me more amenable to your
presence!'

'Then I owe her a great debt,' Thane said solemnly.
'And Michael—will he be as delighted?'

'You're teasing me!' Sapphira regarded him re-
proachfully. 'No, I guess he won't be immediately, but
part of my attraction for him was that I was on his
doorstep and spoke his language. I never encouraged
him, Thane. Whatever he dreamed of was all in his own
mind. I don't doubt for one moment that he'll recover.'

'Well, Athens will prove a happier hunting ground for
him than Kethina, I'm sure,' he commented comfort-
ably. 'Just think of all those tourists—and with the added
cachet of a restaurant destined to become inter-
nationally famous, his stock will be riding pretty high!'

'It was you!' Sapphira shot up on the bed, leaning
over her supine lover, accusation a bright indictment in
her blue eyes. 'You had a hand in their move, because
I've never said anything to you about it.'

'Sapphy...' He reached up a possessive hand.

'No, confess it, you brute!' Horror mingled with admiration in her expression as she refused to surrender to his touch.

Flat on his back, without the dignity of clothes, he still managed to overawe her as he allowed his eyes, still dreamy with pleasure, to travel lethargically over her equally exposed body.

'I may have mentioned the restaurant to Nik Christianides—a hotelier I happened to meet at one of the social events I was called on to attend. He was there alone because his wife was about to give birth to their second child, so we spent some time together. I must admit, he was very interested. When I told him what an excellent reputation it had, he told me he'd make a point of visiting it, because he fancied having an interest in a really top restaurant in Athens.'

'Oh—Thane!' She didn't know whether to laugh or cry. 'How could you? You wanted to get rid of both of them—Lorna and Michael!'

'You make me sound like the Mafia.' He couldn't meet her accusing eyes. 'It was only a suggestion. I wouldn't have forced them out of Kethina even if I'd had the power to do it.' He sighed. 'I'd like to tell you that I saw my recommendation as some kind of expression of gratitude for the friendship they'd given you—but it wouldn't be true. I admit that I believed they were both influencing you against me and I didn't need enemies sitting on my doorstep. I was having a hard enough time as it was. I wanted to find that spark which used to flare between us, and at times that meant being more cruel to you than I liked, particularly because I'm not the most patient or cold-blooded of men—and I didn't need your chaperon waiting in the wings to pluck you away from me!'

Unable to find the words to describe his temerity, Sapphira could only gaze down on his personable face and wonder at his powerful sense of purpose.

'Dear God, Sapphy,' he pleaded, desperation curdling the timbre of his voice, 'I know it was unethical, but they say all is fair in love and war. And it wasn't my decision anyway. If Christianides made the offer, it would be up to Michael West and his partner whether they accepted it or not. It wasn't as if they were being lured to the ends of the earth. Athens is only a taxi ride from here after all...'

She heard the desperation in his voice and smiled.

'But not as easily accessible as if it had been a short walk down the road?' she asked softly.

'No.' He made no excuse.

'Oh, Thane, I should be so angry with you...'

'I didn't mean to deprive you, Sapphy. I meant to fill Lorna's place in your life. To give you support and friendship and understanding...' There was a pause whilst she remained feasting her eyes on his face, seeing the shadow of shame and vulnerability, and aching to appease them both. 'Can you forgive me?'

He deserved to suffer, so she pretended to consider while he watched her, his face taut with expectation.

'Will Lorna be a welcome visitor in this house?' she asked at last.

'Of course,' he agreed unhesitatingly. 'And her brother too—preferably when he is accompanied by his fiancée or wife—if that's what you want.'

It was time to put him out of his misery. 'All I want,' she assured him softly, 'apart from our babies, is you, Thane.'

With a cry of exultation he pulled her down on top of him, and she claimed his body with a satisfaction all the greater because she had come so close to losing him completely.

As his mouth possessed hers with strength and purpose, the remaining words she'd wanted to speak could echo only in her mind—lord, liege—master.

Harlequin Presents®

Coming Next Month

Available in June wherever paperback books are sold, or through Harlequin Reader Service:

In the U.S.
P.O. Box 1397
Buffalo, NY
14240-1397

In Canada
P.O. Box 603
Fort Erie, Ontario
L2A 5X3

Summer Reading At Its Best

In July, Harlequin and Silhouette bring readers the Big Summer Read Program. Heat up your summer with these four exciting new novels by top Harlequin and Silhouette authors.

SOMEWHERE IN TIME by Barbara Bretton
YESTERDAY COMES TOMORROW by Rebecca Flanders
A DAY IN APRIL by Mary Lynn Baxter
LOVE CHILD by Patricia Coughlin

From time travel to fame and fortune, this program offers something for everyone.

Available at your favorite retail outlet.

BSR

OVER THE YEARS, TELEVISION HAS BROUGHT
THE LIVES AND LOVES OF MANY CHARACTERS INTO
YOUR HOMES. NOW HARLEQUIN INTRODUCES YOU
TO THE TOWN AND PEOPLE OF

One small town—twelve terrific love stories.

GREAT READING...GREAT SAVINGS...AND A FABULOUS
FREE GIFT!

Each book set in Tyler is a self-contained love story; together, the
twelve novels stitch the fabric of the community.

By collecting proofs-of-purchase found in each Tyler book, you can
receive a fabulous gift, ABSOLUTELY FREE! And use our special
Tyler coupons to save on your next TYLER book purchase.

Join us for the fourth TYLER book,
MONKEY WRENCH by Nancy Martin.

*Can elderly Rose Atkins successfully bring a new love into
granddaughter Susannah's life?*

"GET AWAY FROM IT ALL" SWEEPSTAKES

HERE'S HOW THE SWEEPSTAKES WORKS

NO PURCHASE NECESSARY

To enter each drawing, complete the appropriate Official Entry Form or a 3" by 5" index card by hand-printing your name, address and phone number and the trip destination that the entry is being submitted for (i.e., Caneel Bay, Canyon Ranch or London and the English Countryside) and mailing it to: Get Away From It All Sweepstakes, P.O. Box 1397, Buffalo, New York 14269-1397.

No responsibility is assumed for lost, late or misdirected mail. Entries must be sent separately with first class postage affixed, and be received by: 4/15/92 for the Caneel Bay Vacation Drawing, 5/15/92 for the Canyon Ranch Vacation Drawing and 6/15/92 for the London and the English Countryside Vacation Drawing. Sweepstakes is open to residents of the U.S. (except Puerto Rico) and Canada, 21 years of age or older as of 5/31/92.

For complete rules send a self-addressed, stamped (WA residents need not affix return postage) envelope to: Get Away From It All Sweepstakes, P.O. Box 4892, Blair, NE 68009.

© 1992 HARLEQUIN ENTERPRISES LTD.   SWP-RLS

"GET AWAY FROM IT ALL" SWEEPSTAKES

HERE'S HOW THE SWEEPSTAKES WORKS

NO PURCHASE NECESSARY

To enter each drawing, complete the appropriate Official Entry Form or a 3" by 5" index card by hand-printing your name, address and phone number and the trip destination that the entry is being submitted for (i.e., Caneel Bay, Canyon Ranch or London and the English Countryside) and mailing it to: Get Away From It All Sweepstakes, P.O. Box 1397, Buffalo, New York 14269-1397.

No responsibility is assumed for lost, late or misdirected mail. Entries must be sent separately with first class postage affixed, and be received by: 4/15/92 for the Caneel Bay Vacation Drawing, 5/15/92 for the Canyon Ranch Vacation Drawing and 6/15/92 for the London and the English Countryside Vacation Drawing. Sweepstakes is open to residents of the U.S. (except Puerto Rico) and Canada, 21 years of age or older as of 5/31/92.

For complete rules send a self-addressed, stamped (WA residents need not affix return postage) envelope to: Get Away From It All Sweepstakes, P.O. Box 4892, Blair, NE 68009.

© 1992 HARLEQUIN ENTERPRISES LTD.   SWP-RLS

Myles Paio

"GET AWAY FROM IT ALL"

Brand-new Subscribers-Only Sweepstakes

OFFICIAL ENTRY FORM

This entry must be received by: April 15, 1992
This month's winner will be notified by: April 30, 1992
Trip must be taken between: May 31, 1992—May 31, 1993

YES, I want to win the Caneel Bay Plantation vacation for two. I understand the prize includes round-trip airfare and the two additional prizes revealed in the BONUS PRIZES insert.

Name _____

Address _____

City _____

State/Prov._____ Zip/Postal Code_____

Daytime phone number _____
(Area Code)

Return entries with invoice in envelope provided. Each book in this shipment has two entry coupons — and the more coupons you enter, the better your chances of winning!
© 1992 HARLEQUIN ENTERPRISES LTD.   1M-CPN

"GET AWAY FROM IT ALL"

Brand-new Subscribers-Only Sweepstakes

OFFICIAL ENTRY FORM

This entry must be received by: April 15, 1992
This month's winner will be notified by: April 30, 1992
Trip must be taken between: May 31, 1992—May 31, 1993

YES, I want to win the Caneel Bay Plantation vacation for two. I understand the prize includes round-trip airfare and the two additional prizes revealed in the BONUS PRIZES insert.

Name _____

Address _____

City _____

State/Prov._____ Zip/Postal Code_____

Daytime phone number _____
(Area Code)

Return entries with invoice in envelope provided. Each book in this shipment has two entry coupons — and the more coupons you enter, the better your chances of winning!
© 1992 HARLEQUIN ENTERPRISES LTD.   1M-CPN